Strongneck Books

Fire

To those who fight and protect us

From these frightful things

Submitter's Note

Hello. My name is Miguel. I myself have not written this book. But instead I received it from my cousin who has asked to remain nameless. He figured that since I work at the Glades Road Library, I probably would better know how to get it published.

My cousin works at Regional Burn Center at Tampa General Hospital and supposedly it happened that a patent died and they were allowed to simply go in and take what they wanted. And he ended up with this book. But I know my cousin. And as such I know that there is a good chance that he has not obtained this manuscript by honest means. As such if you are or know of a rightful heir; please let me know. You can contact me at 561-555-0102

Transcriber's Note

I am a nameless nurse at Regional Burn Center at Tampa General hospital. Or that is I would just assume remain nameless. I am not the writer of this book.

(insert mule picture here)
Houston•Barrow•San Francisco•Upstate New York•Boca Raton

Instead, well there's a dying patent. He has agreed to pay me for this. And I am really having trouble keeping up on my student loan debts. He has decided to explain better.

As for me, I am doing this at a time when I won't get caught. And in order to be sure to stay out of trouble I also will never say who I am.

Author's Note

I am the author of this book. However I am having to dictate it. But please know that this is not a ghost writer. I simply am only able to speak, and with difficulty; all for a reason that will be apparent in time. I have for a long time planned to record my life's work. A chronicle, if you will. But, that is so often the case. We'll lose that weight, we'll write a book, we'll remodel the house. Stuff happens, we procrastinate, we get started and it goes to nowhere for 5 minutes. But not this time. I'm pretty sure that I'm not going to be around for much longer; same reason I need to dictate this whole book including this paragraph right here.

P.S. You should know that I am also having to take a lot of drugs, like morphine. As such any misrememberings and / or errors are the product of pain killers. Not me.

"The natural agency or active principle operative in combustion; popularly conceived as a substance visible in the form of flame or of a ruddy glow or incandesce" – from the definition of fire from The Oxford English Dictionary (c. 1984)

(insert mule picture here)
Houston•Barrow•San Francisco•Upstate New York•Boca Raton

Chapter one

The smoke could be seen blocks away. The others knew that this was going to be a bad fire. A fire for the record books. But not me. This was my first fire. I hadn't been a firefighter a week, and so far all we had responded to was a Life-alert that wasn't even serious, and an honest accident with a fire alarm. But this was no alarm. No geriatric-dementia had picked themselves up off the floor using the fire alarm here. In face there was no fire alarm at all. But there was fire; and so much of it.

The house was the largest in the town; barring those with historical markers. So big was it that they has to halt construction while the homeowner's accusation litigated off what would have been the 3rd floor. It had a media room, a walk in pantry, an almost Olympic sized swimming pool, a 4 car garage, who even knows just how many bedrooms and bathrooms and about whatever else you could ever think of. And a fire. It was on the very edge of the neighborhood, they in fact tried to be out of range of zoning, to make it as big as they wanted no doubt. But by they ended up making legal mistakes and for financial reasons they simply shrank it.

"Fitzgerald!-Pickles! Keep it outa the woods!" "You! I want you inside!" "Kennedy! Hook up the hydrant!"

I didn't understand why a rookie would be going in instead of staying out, manning a hose. But you don't question your superior when you have no seniority, and certainly not when smoke is piling, and you know not everyone's been able to get out.

BASH! Down went the door. It wasn't easy to break down. They had used good screws when they installed the lock. The idea is that a good lock will simply bust through the doorframe in the event of a kick-in invasion. And they're right. Longer screws holding the metal plate in place really do make it hard to break in; and they do make you safer from vandals and burglars. But no one was going to break into this house. Not now. Not ever.

I immediately saw something horrible. I expected it to be black with smoke. It wasn't. Everything was a bright orange-red. Fire covered everything. The floors were on fire. The Swedish plastic furniture was on fire. It was as though a large pitcher of liquid fire had been poured out onto literally everything. Fire may always reach upwards; but nevertheless, even the celling was on fire.

Couldn't have much of anything visual in a firebomb like this; so we used a heat sensing device. The technology was initially used by high-level law enforcement to be able to see people through walls; it was now adapted soasto allow us to find victims in a fire.

Smash! Another firefighter went through the floor trying up the stairs. Wasn't hurt, but showed couldn't go that way. We'd start by searching the ground floor.

They don't build em like they too. Used to houses would be made of wood. Solid beams cut straight from the tree. Furniture would be made of leather, or at least cloth; and, either have a solid wood frame, or simply be made of solid wood. Now solid wood and real leather are luxury options. Ones people can't always find at all. A room built with all old stuff, stuff like that takes a minute to catch. Such a room, it was found by Underwriters' Laboratories, takes 20 minutes to catch. But this was no such room. Clearly these people, like myself, had very modern taste. The couch was made of plastic, and it had burned down the foam. The walls had a foe-brick covering. Real brick won't burn; most it could do would be to have the mortar come undone. But this was no brick; instead it was a plasticized foe-brick. Do doubt resembling the basic structure of foam. It was melting and burning like some face-melting scene. They had a television that I estimated was triple digits in terms of the inches. And quadruple digits in terms of price. I had never seen a burnt TV before. Also they had a bookshelf. Doubt any books were really on it. Just bric-a-brac, mostly resembling books. It was bright and illuminating with fire; It had never been intended for lighting purposes. Only thing on it that was nether on fire nor melted was made of glass. We kept away because were anticipating it's collapse.

We thought we heard someone in the master bedroom. That door had been left open, so in we went. We began searching through the smoke.

"Somebody left the radio on!" shouted another. By which point I had just cleared the adjacent full-bath. Then we went into check the walk-in closet. It was filled with soot black smoke. There is a saying that the tension is so thick you could cut it with a knife; but in this case it wasn't tension. I literally cut the smoke with my hand; slicing it through the air. The room, assuming it could be called such, was packed with, no doubt expensive, clutter. Vegan leather shoes, petroleum based textiles, and other items produced an extremely thick, rich chemically smoke. I could just imagine the thousands of dollars spent at Nordstrom, Sax Fifth Avenue, and Neman Markups, previously a lavish wardrobe. Now going up in smoke; literally. I went to check enclosed storage, sometimes scared children will hide in such places; even though that's the opposite of what they should be doing. Except in reality some foolhardy architect had placed a closet in a closet. Next thing I knew I was on my back.

"DUDE! You hearin' me?!"

"Yeah, yeah, what'd I miss?" I replied.

"Apparently a big boom. But checked through; nobody's here. You good to keep on?"

"Yeah, yeah, let's do this," I lied.

We vacated the closet and went into the gourmet kitchen. First thing I saw was the countertops.

"Concrete; chemicals from having to re-seal them quarterly must be burning off."

SMASH

The bottom fell out of their cabinets, literally. Plastic; no doubt from a kit. An entire set of dishes shattered simultaneously. One of the firefighters clapped.

"Where does that custom come from anyway?" I asked. No one answered; who would in that kind of a fire? I still don't know the answer.

We went into the butler's pantry, but to see we needed to check about body heat. Then the fire chief radioed in. Told us to get out. 30 seconds later we were being talked to by him.

Everyone ok?

"He make a rookie mistake. Ended up flat on his back; not in a-"

"Cut the dirty jokes-" said the fire chief.

"I'm fine," I said.

"Great, everyone else?" he said.

"Didn't a knife fall out and hit you-" said another.

"Who keeps knives in the cabinet?" she replied.

The chief paused and we all did likewise with him for just but a moment.

(insert mule picture here)
Houston•Barrow•San Francisco•Upstate New York•Boca Raton

"I'm fine, didn't stab me or anything like that," she said.

"Good, now those pops we called you out for. Had 2 cars in the garage; but the Tesla and the Jaguar seem both to have finished. When the fire hit the fuel-well-anyways. Need you back up in there. Looks clear."

We went back in. This time the first thing we did was go into what had been a closet. Initially we thought it might have been a bonus room. We were wrong. It was so burnt out we couldn't tell what even had been stored in the closet. But there was what I hesitate to call a door. It was so burnt there was virtually nothing left. I could tell right off the bat it had been made out of powder board. Normal solid wood will not burn like powder board. Normal wood takes time to catch, the outer layers burn, get covered in ash, and insulate the interior of the wood from further combustion. This is also why every fireplace, except those that use gas only, must have a fire poker in order to knock off the ashes so it can finish burning. This process does not occur with powder board. Powder board is exactly what the name implies. It is a board made from ground up powdered wood, glued into retaining whatever shape the carpenter has elected. For starters little bits of wood burn much more than a board; surface area. This is the process behind tinder used to start a campfire. Also if you have ever tried to burn documents; you have seen firsthand how much better a sheet of paper burns, and burns completely, by itself. As opposed to trying to burn a whole book at once. Which is exactly what had happened. Also there is the matter of the glue itself. The glue will also burn in and of itself.

The doorway led into a micro-library. Not to be confused with a give a book-take a book. The walls no doubt had been coated by crammed full bookshelves.

"Oh man, this is got to be what started it,"

There were piles of ashes resembling books everywhere. I worried what obscure and out of print adventures had just been exterminated and lost to the sands of time forever. But there was more. I actually stepped on a piece of metal, and found broken glass. Kerosene lantern. Had to have been. You see, a kerosene lantern is basically the same principal as a monitof cocktail, though intended for a different purpose. Admittedly the cocktail is more dangerous; but they both work much the same way. Both have a glass reservoir on the bottom, as the name implies; usually kerosene, however the cocktail can use most any accelerant. Both have a wick of some kind through which the accelerant-fuel comes up by the soak-through process to be burned. Also the lantern has a second glass chimney surrounding the flame. The cocktail is intended solely as a homemade weapon; and had extensive use in the Russian revolution. The lantern also saw much use in the past; especially before electric lighting. But this one had been knocked over.

I saw a late old man. He was clearly dead. I could only tell he was old because remarkably he still had some gray hair unsigned. What much have happened was one of two things. He had been up late reading and fell asleep and by moving in his sleep knocked the lamp. By the time he woke up he was trapped. Or possibly he simply broke the thing, either way. We knew he was dead. It no doubt was an excruciating death, unless he somehow managed to sleep thought it, which was a possibility. It was a death greatly feared by the Amish; who work in barns filled with flammable hay and use similar lanterns, they drop it. They're dead. Another example is the story of how the great Chicago fire started. A cow kicking over a lantern in a barn; but who knows if it's true. We'd probably never know the circumstances; only indicator was whether or not he was in the chair. But the chair was made with plastic and petro-chemical based foam. It was so consumed I couldn't tell anything about it or from it. We would never know. This horrible scene resembled something from Foxe's book of Martyrs.

(insert mule picture here)
Houston•Barrow•San Francisco•Upstate New York•Boca Raton

"I think we can rule out arson and gas"

It was a strange death. When a house fire takes a life; normally it's just smoke inhalation. Not this time. We finished clearing the ground floor with a hybrid of reverence and simply shock. But the stairs had by that point completely given way, so to get to the upper floor we had to use the latter truck; which by this point had arrived. When we went to go in; we found it to be one of those unbreakable windows. In the training academy the instructor called them neo-burglar bars. Many people in the past had died in fires because they lived in an unsafe neighborhood; and burglar bars were not one way.   It's not something people think about when they buy windows normally. Sure they are good for keeping robbers out. But in a fire they help to keep firemen out, and you in. We got through, but had to take the window out. Never seen anything we couldn't get into; with our equipment, like most fire departments, we could even get into a bank vault.

It was dark with smoke when we entered in; I heard a fellow firefighter stumble over something. I started feeling around and started to see a pattern. We soon realized movie theater seats. It was a media room, didn't guess it at first because the blackout drapes had been consumed. We used heat sensing and found no people were in the media room, at least that had been evacuated.

Smash!

The projector fell out of the celling; narrowly missing a fellow fireman. We were more cautious as we finished clearing the room.

I felt the door; and it started to crumble, what was left. It was hot on the other side, so we needed another way out, and soon because it was going to fall apart and equivalently open itself. As we were climbing back out the way we came in, I was proven right. It was a safe bet that all windows we would have to stop and remove rather than simply break, and now it was already open. We found our way out into a smoky hallway, and a large piece of drywall had fallen off revealing the studs. It was no surprise to find that this house had been built out of pressed wood. I have already gone into detail to explain how that was bad. Lots of flammable glue to burn. Nowadays most of the time people may say something burned to the ground, but usually it merely burns up, burns out, not burns down literally to the ground. But this would be an exception; this was built purely using modern and engineered materials. This would burn to the ground.

We came to the first door we found, and it wasn't hot on the other side. Maybe the fire hadn't reached this room? Immediately as soon as we opened the door, the already very smoky hallway began to fill with rich thick smoke. Also I heard the air conditioner come on. It confused me; first why bother with an air conditioner under circumstances such as these? Second, why didn't it realize it was way too hot in here earlier? Neither made sense. But with all this smoke; might help to set some of it out.

Once I entered the room, the first thing I saw was an Amazon Fire sitting out, no doubt ruined. Irony, whatdaya gunu do?

Then I saw what had happened. Children laying strewn lying about the floor; it must have been a sleepover. They weren't in their sleeping bags. They had woken up, In fact I saw the fire escape latter sitting out. Maybe it was left out, but I doubt it. They were trying to get out. Maybe they felt the door and it was hot; maybe not. Likely they found the stairs out. I knew two things. First we had to get them out and to an ambulance now. Second; there may be more.

It was radioed in, and after we were able to break through the window they were taken down by way of the latter truck. Then we were proceeding onto search the rest of the second floor. All the time I could barely pay attention. Besides being bruised and hurting from earlier; I couldn't stop imagining what it must have been like. Waking up, no doubt to screams of panic. Taking a breath and getting lungs full of smoke. Automatically coughing out the smoke, to soon come to the realization that there is no air, nothing but smoke, unlimited smoke. All the air there was what you had and breathed out without thinking. All while your eyes are burning like acid from all the smoke. A frightening experience for even an adult; but terrifying and traumatizing to a child. Realizing what was happening and then groping to find your way out; just to burn yourself trying to fell around. Realizing that you simply must get out, but being absolutely powerless to do anything to survive, being in a hopeless situation. In a panic reaching for your teddy bear and burning yourself on the crumbling ashes that were your teddy bear. Realizing you can't just go downstairs, or scream for a parent like any normal night; trying to remember what you didn't pay attention to in fire safety. Instead making a panicked scramble for escape with blistered and scalded hands. Or simply trying to stick your head out the window for air. In both synereos realizing you can't get the window open. You can't get out. The panicked screams; maybe they're from you; who knows? Who cares? The high squeal of the fire alarm. The Fire Alarm! I haven't heard a fire alarm. Seeing everything you treasure light up in flames; the only light to prevent total blackens. Though with what the smoke does to your eyes; might not be able to see it.

We ended up finding the hatch to the attic open; so we had to search there. Maybe one climbed up onto the roof for safety; or at least tried. Course how they could reach the pull was beyond me. The fold-up-fold-down latter collapsed under the weight of the first one up. We boosted ourselves up. Somehow it was more full of richer-thicker smoke. I wasn't sure if it was simply up, thus where the smoke would rise to. Or cheap insulation made from materials you can't pronounce. Probably both. The smoke was so thick no one would have much of a chance of surviving. So we didn't make that close a search for victims. I worried that we would miss someone; but I didn't question orders. If there was a way to escape, hopefully the found it and were relatively safe on the roof.

We got out the same way the children did. We were absolutely exhausted, and our air tanks depleted. Not five minutes were we out when they were calling everyone out. They couldn't finish their more thorough search of the attic. It about to implode any time now. By this time new crews already on scene doing a breaking news bulletin interrupting I Love Lucy on insomniac theater.

"So, this is my new line of work."

"Yup," he said taking a breath from his grape Poweraide.

"Guess I can cancel my gym membership," I said.

"You think?"

"Well, I mean"

"Oh I don't know, How do you think I made it into the firefighter's calendar?"

"But you didn't make it into the summer months," I said.

"What's that supposed to mean?" He snapped back.

"It means that we're tired of listening to you bragging incessantly like you're 13 years old!" she said.

"Yeah!" I said "Say, you ok after that knife thing?"

"It's, It's nothing,"

"I don't believe this! And you! You've been here 3-"

"4," I said, "Midnight passed."

"Exactly! And You!, ... You! ... I'll get back to you. But You! You haven't been here 96 hours-"

"Time enough, and the press is here. Try not to make us all look like bicep brains"

"Here comes the boss" he said.

"Hi everything going good on your end?" said the chief.

"Yeah, I'm worried she's slightly injured. But basically, all things being equal, yes." I said

"Bradley Manning" she said.

"Brian Williams," I replied.

"Guys! Stop calling each other references I don't get!" said the boss.

We were interrupted in our squabble by the house imploding. It stayed a roaring fire.

The boss came back soon to say "Hydrants been opened up for regular maintenance. City didn't bother to bring them back online after they were done. Took all hands that we had to keep it out of the woods. Some trees had to come down, 3-4 spot fires started in brush, but we were able to stop it. I'm somewhat surprised that we were able to keep it in. House probably couldn't have been saved no matter what; even still got water to run hoses for just a few minutes, but the house was such a loss I decided to save what water we do have in case it jumps the fire break. Guess less for waste management to haul off this way."

The look on his face I didn't at first recognize; but as I obtained seniority, I in time would come to not only recognize that face; but to know it far better I would ever even imagine to even want to know it.

"Lot of polymers in there. Cheap neo-materials. Like the MGM Grand Hotel Fire in Vegas. I remember that story giving me nightmares. Look, I may have experience as a firefighter. But I'm new at being the boss.   Can't help but blame myself for this-"

"Lota plastic got burnt up, it's just a house."

"Yeah, and with a poppus exterior at that, and a media room, and pool-" she said.

"House, Smouse, give me a mouse. It's not about the house. Those kids," said the boss.

"You heard about that?" he said.

"Of course word got to me; I'm the boss! They're not going to be ok,"

"Did one of them actually die?" I said.

"They all did"

"*Substance capable of undergoing a rapid chemical change to produce hot gases which occupy a much greater volume, and therefore exert a very high pressure*" – From the Entry for Explosives from The Penguin Encyclopedia

(insert mule picture here)
Houston•Barrow•San Francisco•Upstate New York•Boca Raton

Chapter Two

By all rights, my very first fire was when I was 18. At this point I had not become a firefighter; rather I was still a collage student. Undeclared in my major, having not even decided what to do with my life.

I had come home from collage for Thanksgiving. The house smelled of turkey, gravy, and the foods associated with thanksgiving. My uncles were all couching hard watching the game. With the exception of having come home for thanksgiving from collage for the first time it was a pretty normal Thanksgiving. Everyone with their mind on one thing and one thing alone. Food.

I had decided to step outside into the garden. Just for a moment. I was looking out at the yard, seeing how little had changed. About all that had changed was weeding was now insufficient now that I was not here providing chores. I worried if I would be sent to do it just this once while I was still home.

Then the event happened. I jumped when I heard the sound. Could just have easily believed it to have been celebratory cannon fire. In my double take out-of-the-corner-of-my-eye glance, thought I saw it shooting up into the air. It scared me. Then I heard the cries. Screams of fear and pain and agony. All but automatically I jumped the fence. As much as anything rushing in before my family could tell me not to. I stepped in the garden fountain to give myself a boost, then I put my hand on top of the fence to thrust myself over like some guy on a TV at Journey's. But, I'm not the most athletic, and I burned my hand on the fence and came crashing down on the other side. Epic fail.

Then I saw it. All around me. Everywhere. Fire. Everything was on fire and fire was everywhere. People were screaming. Trying and scrambling to find some way to put it out. For only a moment I forgot and thought that I had actually found my way in to Hell. But, then I remembered.

They were rushing, I couldn't see features. But I knew this was the townhouse next door. And I imagined that this was a family having gotten together. But now they were on fire. They screamed and cried out for help.

I saw a ring of plastic chairs, they must have been sitting around. But now the chairs were melting, almost dissolving. I even saw something I had never seen anywhere (including the internet) before or to this day. Fire shadows. Parts of the chair were protected from them sitting there and as such were void of fire instead of void of light.

I saw clearly what had obviously happened. A large cookout propane burner, a big cook pot, carpenter's clamps. Every year millions of Americans decide to fry their turkey. Hundreds of which succeed in setting their house on fire, and 5 people die. That's why if you go that option, the turkey must not only be completely thawed, but dry. Otherwise the water will make the grease boil hard, boil over. Naturally you will be using some form of gas powered apparatus; such as here. And the spill-over will ignite, and lead the fire right into the pot. That much grease burning will be out of control. This here was the opposite of what to do. They had not even bothered to thaw the Turkey. So they made sure it went into cold oil (at least not boiling). Which is actually worse. When it heats up, ice melts. And it will boil over worse than ever. Utterly out of control. But this real genius decided he would just hold it all in. And used carpentry clamps to hold the lid down and stop that from happening. Problem was this wasn't a pressure cooker. (Nor do I know if you even can use grease in a pressure cooker) Pressure and heat had just built up and up. Probably thought it was a cleaver hack to cook the turkey quick. But with no means of escape. It eventually just blew up. Splattering hot scalding grease everywhere in every direction. By the time I had jumped the fence it had all ignited.

It took me a minute to get my wits about me. Realize what had to be done. It was hard to tell what things were, or perhaps on second thought, what things had been might be a more appropriate tense. I soon found a garden hose to put it out.

"Yeowch!" the hose was on fire. I realized I could smell it burning. The shrubs were burning. Other more horrific things were burning. Even the cement was burning! I would later realize it had to have been splattered grease burning.

I didn't know what to do. "STOP DROP AND ROLL!!" I yelled. However I was barely heard over all the screams. Also I wasn't the first to have the idea.

I didn't know how to save them. I kept looking for something to save them. Then it hit me. There, right in the epicenter of it. Was a big 5 gal. canister of propane fuel.

"GET BACK IT'S GOING TO BLOW!!!" I screamed. And not a moment off. Almost as if a commander ordering FIRE! It went off. Much to surprise, not a massive explosion to finish them off. Rather I first realized a sound like a jet plane taking off. But, despite the inferno encompassing the entire area; and it being in the epicenter. I nevertheless could see the flame-thrower like flame coming off the tank.

I didn't know what to do. All this had happened in a matter of moments. They were trying to beat it out; but oil doesn't go out easily. Then I realized it. Everything was on fire, including me. I felt my legs getting excruciatingly hot. To this day I am glad for my (I do admit; rather preposterous) rapper phase. I was able to yank off my tank top in a moment. Even faster were by baggy pants able come off, even over my shoes. I didn't feel any pain, but I knew that actually was a bad sign; I figured I'd deal with it later. (later I would discover I actually had gotten my clothes of fast enough they I didn't get a burn.)

Not knowing what else to do I rushed inside hoping to find something to put them out. Not even fully sure myself if I was on fire; figured I'd find out soon enough. The handle to the sliding glass door had burning oil on it. So I quickly found a rock (one that was mostly not on fire. Grabbing it by the oil free portion I slammed it through the glass. Fortunately it was the kind that broke on contact. It easily broke into tiny pieces, resembling crushed café ice more than actual shards. The hole wasn't nearly big enough for me to escape inside through. So I put in a second hole, then I was able to reach in and open it from the inside. Carelessly I disposed of the rock. And quickly yanked the door open. Immediately once inside I felt a major blast of cold (by comparison). I shed my partially melted shoes (post panic I would be sad for they were nearly $750).

The first thing I did was scramble to find an extinguisher. I didn't think the kitchen sink sprayer would be able to stretch far enough. Then I heard a baby crying; screaming. What was happening outside was so horrible I hesitated slightly. But surely other people would have heard the blast. My family would no doubt do something. But, who that wouldn't be in critical condition knew the baby was there? The townhouse was no doubt going to ignite. I tore up the stairs. Which I knew where they were from having been there before in the townhouse under different neighbors. In my albeit short scramble I heard the smoke alarms going off. Figured it was simply siding on fire, took it as was to be expected and gave it no more thought.

Little did I know…

It really was a small residence, so I was able to tell which of the two bedrooms it had to be where the crying was coming from. I dashed in there, shoving aside the ajar door. At this point mostly just worried about stuff falling on me. No offence to my former neighbors; but the place really was a mess; and the upper floor was worse. But, how was I glad that I had dashed up there. Because in the crib, in the explosion something had gotten in. The first thing I saw was the bedding on fire. The baby was screaming. As fast as I could I snatched the baby from the crib and beat out the fire, careful not to bruise as I could. It was a onesy with snaps so I was able to quickly and easily pull off the burnt clothing. I looked close. The diaper hadn't ignited, good. Course, as I look back. I don't know if the baby's clothes ever were on fire, at least not for certain. It is required for children's pajamas to be fire retardant. Nevertheless there was a fire in that room; that I can confirm. I momentarily paused only to make sure no other infants were in the room. Then dashed out; expecting the whole place to be engulfed in fire all but momentarily.

I didn't even bother trying to put it out. What was the point? Between what had to be happening outside and the siding I knew to be on fire. What was the point?

I stuck my head in the master bedroom and screamed "ANYONE IN THERE?" Squat. Crickets. All this time I had been hearing the shouts of pain, and terror, and panic. I dashed down the stairs and let myself out the front. I had planned to go out a window if I had to hunt out a key; but fortunately the door opened and locked keylessly on the inside. My first real break of the day. As I ran from that door (which I didn't even bother shutting) back next door to help with response, it was only then that it occurred to me. Broken glass. For myself (like with being on fire) if me I'd be knowing about it soon enough. But the baby? I had been in such a rush I had never bothered even trying to figure out gender. Didn't care. Well, I hadn't seen any blood. Figured someone else could check closer. I also knew, with all the people coming and going we hadn't even bothered to lock our front door, much the same as while bringing in groceries. Another break. I dashed in the front, ringing the bell to announce myself.

First thing I did when I got inside was I handed the baby off to my very surprised kid cousin. "Here, check for broken glass." Figured with all she played with dolls, maybe she could handle a real one. Also she just happened to be the most convenient person to hand off to.

Then something clicked with me. I checked. Good I hadn't gone commando. Shieh What was wrong with me? People are on fire and I'm worried about being naked.

I rushed out the back as fast as I could. Knowing that the full weight of the crisis would hit me once again. When I got there I found that my father had gotten his axe and I had been gone so briefly he was still breaking down the fence. Admittedly to save me. He did a double take, so I said "Hurry! Keep At It!" I ran into the house and back just as fast with the kitchen extinguisher. I moment later he had enough of the fence gone they were getting into our yard. The first one through I sprayed. Worried would we have enough foam. Didn't work. He screamed in panic. "CURSES!" I yelled throwing it to the ground. "Type A" I noticed as it dented the garden soil. Should've gotten an "ABC" multi-purpose extinguisher. I knew so when we got it, but at the time I had simply wanted to not get fussed at by fussing.

My mother had apparently gotten a drapery. While I would have expected it to simply burst into flames, it smothered the fire (how maternal). Guess that's why they used to not just have fire extinguishers; but fire blankets. Even would have a little hole to stick a finger in and inspect it much the same as checking the pressure on a fire extinguisher.

The next was a child who jumped into my kid sister and her-probably-really-just-a-friend-who's-a-boy's mud puddle. For all Mom was furious about messing up that corner of her beautiful garden. It really did save the day. Dried mud is peat, peat burns like coal. But this was still wet and messy. In fact this wasn't even the first time my sister's mud had saved the day. In fact a couple years before I left home. A sauté skillet ignited. Mom was in the restroom; found out ex-post-facto. Dad was scrambling to find the lid. And in came sis with Sebastian filthy as two 5 years olds can be (pretty dirty).

"'Look! We made mud pies!' she said."

"'THANK YOU!' I shouted in a scramble."

I threw globs of mud at the fire. The mess was horrible; but our home was saved. That was also how we got the formentioned extinguisher.

Two others followed suit and jumped in the mud. Another extended reiatives were able to smother with dirt. And the 6th was put out the same way as the first by my mother.

And they were out. I breathed a sigh of relief.

"They're still heated to that temperature. They're still cooking!" said an uncle.

"Hurry! Bring water from the kitchen!" said an aunt.

Thinking more clearly my sister grabbed the hose, the same one her and the twice formentioned boy used to make mud, make messes, and irritate mom. And she sprayed them. The blast was a large, encompassing spray thanks to the attachment. Being November, and living up north, the water was good and cold.

"Done," she said.

And just like that. It was done. It's doubtful that all that took much more than a minute. (judging by the yam's timer). And then I looked around. There was a hole in the neighbor's fence. The yard was on fire. The neighbor's townhouse was on fire.

Soon any minute the fire would reach and spread to ours. In that I was glad that I had deliberately flunked that collage entrance exam so I could go to school far enough away to justify a dormitory. Also I realized it was cold.

The fire! The neighbor's yard! The injured! They were bad burned. They would definitely have to be taken to intensive care. I started to check to see about belts, clothing, rings… I knew that much first aid.

"No don't! it might come off with their charred flesh!" an uncle shouted.

I knew he was right. But, I didn't know what to do. I noticed that not all of them were charred; much as how those chairs, parts were shielded. I also noticed the fence. It was completely on fire. Even some of our shrubs had ignited. We had to get them out.

Dad went in to get the key to the rear gate in the back of the garden. We would take them out past the parking area. Away from the cars. Get them to a safe place.

I didn't know really how to move an injured person. So I simply was careful and tried to not do any further injury. As we started to move one I heard an aunt say "No! No! go back!" before I could ask why I heard an explosion. A tiny convertible had been parked near the fence. It had ignited.

"Oh, it's already blown up!" I said.

At the time I may have not gone through firefighter's training. But she, and everyone else knew we were going to have our garden go up. The hose couldn't stop that (although some attempt was made) but even our house was going to burn. Which was also the same reason we couldn't take them inside.

We went past the burning vehicle, with one car between us. Like most modern cars it was built with lightweight materials for mileage reasons. I coughed and choked on the toxic smoke. We put him down on the far side of the driveway. We didn't put him on the grass for fear of burs and other natural stuff. It was thin forest – wilderness as much as anything. My aunt stayed with him and began (as best she could) shock treatment.

I ran back to the gate as fast as I could, holding my breath as I passed it.

"WHAT! WHY AREN'T YOU ALL CARRYING MORE!!" I blurted.

"You out of breath, you ok?" said my mom.

"NEVER MIND THAT. –" I said.

"Going through the cars, should take them up front-"

"Easier for fire engines to get to them up front, besides, the collective yard up front. It could burn," I said. I'll just tell you that it had a lot of trees, especially for what it was.

"You know, come to think of it. I probably should move my car," said my uncle.

The look my father gave him.

"Ok, but make it quick, they may all go!" he said.

"Say, that reminds me. Shouldn't we call the fire department?" I said.

"The road to Hell is paved with good intensions" - American Proverb

Chapter Three

After that horrific experience I had decided I was going to be a firefighter. I still remember how surprised I was they all survived. I wouldn't say they were ok, but they did survive. I didn't know how anyone could survive that. But, in 9/11 there was someone in the pentagon who was drenched in burning jet fuel. And naturally stop, drop, and roll didn't work. But, of all his co-workers. Only he survived.

After all that I found out and signed up for the appropriate classes that would help me when I returned to collage. I got more serious and after graduation I shaved my facial hair and signed up at the fireman's academy. Wasn't at the very top of the class. But I did well. Certainly wasn't at the bottom. On the book learning, I excelled; even had other classmates coming to me to help them study. But the physical training was more difficult. Nevertheless I graduated full-fledged. And the rest as they say is history.

(insert fire and flames here)

The day started out so normally. I had just begun to settle into Madison FD. We were responding to call about a transformer fire. You know those things on top of power poles. Well the coolant they use is flammable. It's from petroleum and flammable enough so that I've heard of it being used as tractor fuel.

We didn't know what exactly had caused it; but we figured that it was some form of internal problem. Regardless it had already blown up by the time we arrived. Trees had been trimmed back so there wasn't much concern even of something like that.

It was a calm neighborhood. I would even say tranquil. So when we heard shots ring out. It wasn't exactly like a big shocker. Instead it was like "what was that?" Deal was, we didn't even think it was shots. But we certainly didn't know what it was. When we arrived the fire itself had been little to nothing even when we arrived. And now everything had even been hosed off. So we were able to make quick work of getting over there. To this day regret not having nagged the chuffer for us to wrap it up quick. But I didn't. I honestly didn't know. We honestly didn't know. We would never have guessed; could never have guessed. We never heard further shots. We had packed it up and had only gone two blocks when we got the call. In all honestly, it was probably the most convenient timing in my entire career. Not good timing; let's keep that clear. Anything but. However, it was convenient timing. We were actually even closer, than when we were first responding. All we had to do was loop around up a side street. When we got there, there were already plenty of police on scene.

We were shown inside. And what I saw still makes me mad when I think about it. I don't like getting that mad, that kind of mad. What I had already seen. My first fire was simply an accident. My very first fire was the product of sheer stupidity. But this, this I can best describe with only one word. Selfishness.

I saw a teenage boy, older old enough my might have actually been 20. Little younger than I am. He was sprawled out on the floor. There was blood spewed, he had clearly thrown up blood. And he was in handcuffs. He had been shot twice. Naturally we tried to revive him; defibulator, artificial respiration, the works. We cut his shirt off to get to what happened. But, EKG showed squat. And so did everything else. It was obvious he didn't die instantly. I was cross-trained as a paramedic, so I had a pretty good idea what had been hit. The pericardium and a lung. We did what we could. Sure the ambulance came, but that was later. The ambulance driver was the one to formally declare him dead. The paramedics didn't even bother to take him to a trauma center.

It was shocking, it was horrifying. I had heard of corruption and brutality. But, this? It was surprising, awakening to even hear. But to be there, to see it first-hand. Well that's another matter altogether.

(insert fire and flames here)

When we got back to the fire station, like usual we hung up our helmets (in this case figuratively) and plopped down onto the couch (literally). But, this was a tad different. I imagine when surgeons at Loma Linda or Saint Jude's children's hospital loose a patent on the operating table. They too (even if it truly and completely wasn't their fault) can't just call it another day another dollar and punch out the same.

"Wow," I said.

"Yeah" she said.

"These calls dude, they get to you," he said.

In walked the lieutenant / station officer. A.K.A. the boss.

"Well, certainly surprising," he said.

I turned to him and said "Surprising! Try Staggering!" As you probably can guess; I was in a pretty foul mood.

He paused and said "You get used to the things you see."

Now that was frightening.

I visually displayed that to be a disgusting thought.

(insert mule picture here)
Houston•Barrow•San Francisco•Upstate New York•Boca Raton

"Hey! We need police. If someone's breaking into your house, if someone's chasing you at gunpoint. Who are you going to call? Your mommy?"

"Ghostbusters," I couldn't resist.

"Look, just the other day a-" said the boss.

"Let me guess, some cop saved someone somewhere. Yeah, I get it" said my co-worker, "Look, yeah. We need police. It's a necessary part of society; let's just take that as a prerequisite. Not that we got that out of the way, can we please get to the point. They're people, they're imperfect-" he said.

"In any profession, there are bad people. There are some bad lawyers, there are some bad doctors. But look at what they do; and then look at the purge movies. Anarchy-"

"The statement assumes it to be mutually exclusive," she said.

"What?" he said.

"I mean, you're assuming it's not possible to be a hero and a monster at the exact same time," she said, then looked directly at me and said, "How do you think you got your job?"

"Well, firehouse 13 was built to fill a major gap in the city's far west side-"

"No bozo. Why were you the one to get the gig?" she said.

"Well I, I, I was glad to be hired, so-" I said.

"You didn't ask why you?" he said.

She sighed and said, "Because, they were planning originally to have it partially - staffed by transfers. But, one awaiting promotion. Well, one day he pulled a kid out of a major house fire. And then molested the kid. Yeah. He did it again; and now he's in jail where he belongs."

That took me by surprise. Then the boss said "And I got his position."

Eventually I said "Whoa-"

"But! But this is different. Look, ok you admit. You admit that they're, that they are necessary. That the do heroic acts. But, come on. They don't want to get killed; they just want to be able to go home to their families-" said the boss.

"Exactly! And it had been said that the root of all evil is being willing to do anything to get what you want," he said.

"I don't know about that. I believe that evil is like dark and cold. Not something of itself, rather an absence. Albert Einstein described evil as a void of God. But I do believe you have a point. That phrase doesn't say that that something is actually a bad thing, at least of itself. There has got to be a line. There has got to be a point wherein you say that you will not cross. Yes, I know there are exceptions. There are always some extreme, some exception. Some absolute that would truly justify most anything, Course there is also the issue of normalizing and commonplaceifying-" I said.

"They found 3 bricks of-" said the boss.

"Maybe they were simply illegally renting out a room to someone. Who knows? I remember not 2 weeks ago hearing you going on about your cousin losing his tourist-tour's boat because one of the passengers happened to come on board with drugs," I said.

"Yeah, they found that the gun he had, the safety hadn't been turned off," she said.

"HE HAD A GUN!!!-" said the boss.

"Oh come on. The body armor they had. What's it going to do, bruise them?" I said.

"Actually I saw them with a big metal shield they had up front in the raid. So any resistance would have been utterly hopeless," he said.

"They Did!" I said shocked, "In that case what difference does it make if they do get shot?! Furthermore, there are criminals that dress up as cops, and what they were wearing just said 'police.' Most likely, or at least was a good chance was bogus. Wasn't, but could have been."

"It's called a no-knock-raid. As the name implies, they just storm in, like it's a battlefield. Even was a major city that created a video about how to survive a mass shooting. Was good and creepy. And one of the things they said, among others. Was tips on how to get the initially responding officers to not shoot you." he said, sounding surprisingly smart for him.

"You know, this is so like you. You're of such an authoritarian mindset. And, I don't mean like being a controlling person. Rather, like you're just of that. You're just like you're supposed to. Sure you expect that of others, but, more so. It's like, it's like,-"

"No, this is like you. And when I was a teen. I was a lot like you. Rebellious. Got into trouble. Thank God my parents inspected me and found the stuff hidden in my room. They sent me off to military school, and the smacked the smart right out of me," said the boss.

I had known from the first time I met him that I didn't like him. And I had been getting closer and closer to being able to put my finger on it. Now, I knew why.

"What happened to you?" I said.

"They straightened me up," he said, not getting the full weight of concern in my voice.

"No I mean, I mean-" I said, trying to not sound like someone that's trying to think up a new lie by saying the same thing over and over again, "What I mean is I want to speak to the real you. The you, that you really are. Not the predetermined and transplanted person you have been turned into against your will."

"I was involved in drugs! I needed to be straightened out. Look now! Look how far I have come-" he said.

"And that makes it ok!?! It's not making a child deathly ill with chemotherapy hoping to save their life. Just because it turns out well; and the end product is good; does not make it right! Look, look at blacks in the 1950s, pre-and-through-civil-rights-era. They were hard working, they had strong families. They were industrious, and Godly. They were working to climb out of their current place. But, does that make what they went through ok?! OF COURSE NOT Naturally I assume that I need not even bother explaining why. Another example. Charles Dickens; probably one of the greatest British authors of all time; second only to Shakespeare. Sure his stuff's hard to read; but all 20 of his books have never been out of print. But, what shaped him most, probably was having to work at a factory, one that wasn't a good work environment to begin with, because his father was in debtor's prison and his family needed to eat. Instead of going to school. But, there was exploitation of workers, child labor, poor conditions, it was not a good thing. It wasn't ok and shouldn't have happened," I said.

He was shocked. He struck back saying "That is completely different-"

I interrupted and said "How!? Because it was done with good intensions? Because they meant well? That makes it ok? Frankly that's worse. I'll give an example. In the middle ages people were kept from eating tomatoes because they were through to be poison. But if they hadn't been then that probably would have prevented a lot of cases of scurvy. Sure the act itself has an excuse, I mean surely it's not as sinful when you honestly mean well. But also, if it wasn't with good intensions it surely would be easier to see it as it is. But this way, things are perverted. Guilt and conscience, under normal circumstances would lead to the good and right. But here they have been twisted such that they are a point on the spear. A bully just wants to have some fun. But this, this feels a need, an entitlement to get it's grubby little paws on your core being. Let's talk turkey boss; you may have a legitimate excuse, undeniably there are fingers and blame to be pointed. But now you're" (he'd rather me not say just how old he is) "You're emancipated. Now are you going to just continue to sit down and shut up? You don't even have anything to worry about, except for some boo-hoos from your mom which I would promptly hang up on. Are you just going to be 'good' or will you stand up, and will you be liberated?!" I said.

He may not have had his mind changed; but, he did know that he had lost the deliberation. But, his mind had not been changed.

Not yet.

"*War is Hell*" - American Proverb

Chapter Four

(insert mule picture here)
Houston•Barrow•San Francisco•Upstate New York•Boca Raton

I had thought that I had seen the worst there was to see. It had been shocking. It had been horrifying. It had been the tip of the iceberg.

(insert fire and flames here)

A tomboy jumped in the mud. She was glad to be finally having some joy, some enjoyment. These past weeks. Like oh so very many, she had given up so very much. All freedom, most all enjoyment. Just grounding and more grounding, and eventually an explosion would be inevitable. And the response for when that was too much. More grounding. Like most, there had gone all relationship with her parents. She was powerless, she missed her brother.

"GET OUT OF THE MUD!!!" her mother yelled "PUT THAT WORM DOWN"

Most miserably, she came inside. She tried to hide her pain. The adults just couldn't look the other way. They just wouldn't.

(insert fire and flames here)

A young boy was taken back to his cell. God he hated this place. He just needed to escape. TO BREATHE! He was powerless. In all honestly, he was powerless to his parents too. But, though in confidence he would have best and honestly described them as "well meaning." But, here, just as a gun is the opposite of a tax return. This was the opposite of love. He wore the traditional orange jumpsuit. Why? What was the reason? In a community confinement center near, "*San Diego was it?*' they wore street clothes. And that place was adults, and some pretty serious stuff, like murderers. He had thought that school uniforms were bad. But this? The idea in school had been, that that way, their wouldn't be bullying over clothes. That proved to be a load of politician. They just found different things to bully over. Parents praised it because then they didn't argue about what to wear. But, contrary to claims, the school was not co-parenting. That should be something the parents handle themselves. Furthermore, should parents have that much power to begin with? Oh, not that it didn't matter, but what does it matter? He was so far beyond what had happened then. Who knows, eventually he would be released. And then he'd be powerless to his parents again. God would it ever end? What would he be turned into by then? He was afraid of simply having his spirit broken by then. Btu his main fear was actually what he was turning into. Not being made into but rather, an equal and opposite reaction taking him farther the other way. Farther than even he thought to be a good thing. He tried to district himself from his powerlessness. He tried to think of the good times, the bad just made him mad. Anger wasn't safe here.

(insert fire and flames here)

We were stationed at a different firehouse than usual. It wasn't the first time. We had manned a small volunteer firehouse before. Deal was then that they were off fighting a wildfire and we were at their station so the area wouldn't otherwise be void of emergency fire services. But this was virtually unheard of. We instead had come into town to maintain a more urban firehouse. We had even brought our fire engine. Why were we coming into town to be stationed? Because most all fire officials were off on on-site standby. Waiting for the shot heard round the world. While everyone else was holding their breath, so were we. But, for us it was a little different. Already an agreement had been made. No matter what, firefighters and paramedics were and would be neutral. We would take no side. We would have no preferential treatment. And each side would treat us was neutral and be assured that we were not working with or spying for their enemy. But we held our breath. This was the epi-center. All that had gone on for so many weeks, not just here but throughout the land. Our backyard would be the epi-center. Also we were afraid that one of us would break treaty. Sure we all had sides we were hoping for, not to name names but in some cases it was quite obvious. But we put that aside. Even Cooter Brown probably had rooted for one side in the civil war deep down. Thought naturally, the ultimate hope was peace. Unfortunately, that hope was one that would not come to be.

(insert fire and flames here)

There she was. Ready to fight, she had been fighting. But, now, this was different. This was not the weapons of peace. Everything was different. She had to breathe through a homemade gas mask she had heard instructions on how to make because of all the tear gas being unleashed. (Two carpentry masks with crunched charcoal from health food store removed from capsule and coating in between the two) She was afraid that they would come along, and rip off her mask and expose her. God she could barely see! She wished she had a gas scarf to wrap around her head. Sure was cold enough. But no, she would never surrender. It occurred to her, she had heard the expression "fighting on the front lines". Well, she was in front; she could clearly see the police. She was LITERALLY on the front lines. "DO NOT LIGHT YOUR COCKTAIL YET! WAIT TO LIGHT" she heard a leader shouting "PLEASE DO NOT WASTE FUEL. WAIT TO LIGHT"

(insert mule picture here)
Houston•Barrow•San Francisco•Upstate New York•Boca Raton

Then things changed, time passed. The battle began. They took off running; she never got to the lines. The bullet slammed into the frontal lobe; severed her corpus callosum disconnecting the two hemispheres of her brain. Then it shot out over her cerebellum, bursting out the back of her skull. She hit the ground with a thud, the inertia from her running effecting the fall more than the gunshot itself. Like most she was armed with a monitof cocktail. It broke when she hit the ground, bursting into a fire, burning her hand and wrist. She never felt a thing. But, like oh so very many others, she was a shield. At least for a moment. Thereby protecting others, so they could get up close to break through blue lines and barricades.

(insert fire and flames here)

The young boy choked and blinked at the smoke. He should never have told himself it couldn't get any worse. It always can. Oh man! He had even gotten bold and yelled out, shouting for help. He could hear he wasn't the only one. They had to let him out. Surely they would let him out. They had to let him out? Right? And he was right. They did have to let him out. But just as can and should are not the same, nor are have to and will do. He coughed, again. He knew enough to keep low. He started to take his clothes off. He thought, "maybe I can stop up the door, and block it out". And so he tried, he what he could to block it. Which was by far not much.

He perceived more. There was more then, than just his cell, and what was in it. There were more people there. And a light! Oh that light! It, it was the opposite of this horrible place- wait. Isn't this the cliché near death experience? Probably just a dream. But, maybe an escape dream. He looked down. He saw himself laying in the floor. Ut

(insert mule picture here)

oh. Then in walked his younger sister. Like usual, covered in mud. His sister was in the cell with him!

"Wait, are we, like, dead?" he said.

"Fraid so," she replied.

He took her hand, and like that; they were gone.

(insert fire and flames here)

The first sign we got was the sound of a jet crashing down in a park, not terribly near even our firehouse. But, it was very loud. While most of America was sitting by the TV, much like as they were on 9/11. We weren't. We were, almost, too prepared to even watch TV. Expecting what probably would be the greatest, or should I say worst call of all our careers. At all times in a firehouse, we're on call. Ready and waiting for something to happen. But this time we were super-uber prepared. We even knew what the call was going to be. Or so we thought. A plane coming out of the sky?! That was worse than we had even imagined. At that the boss finally decided that we would go in without being called in.

And what I found. What we saw. It was horrible.

On the way, like a block away. We passed another place crash. Confirming our fears that it was in fact an air force plane. It had crashed onto parallel parking, bystanders were simply trying to keep it from spreading to the adjacent building. We didn't stop to fight the fire. It was beginning to rain, I said "Nice touch." I was glared at by all (including the apparatus engineer who was driving) for belittling the situation. We actually were able to smell it before we could see it. The air stank of blood, and of burnt… everything. In what normally is a busy part of the city. Now was filled with bodies. Firefighters were already busily tending to the injured, which were everywhere. Probably what few were unscathed were already gone from here (police and otherwise). I have heard in Gettysburg, and similar battles, the army surgeons would go around simply seeing who they thought they could save. Same here. The station itself was all ablaze, it had even taken a hit from a fighter jet. Out of a squadron of 5, the forth hit a parking garage nearby. And the fifth got away. Also adjacent buildings had gunshot wound victims. At least one (I forget how many if others as well) also had a fire in them. But the fire fighters were concentrating simply to those in the street. Merely the highest concentration. And so many injured, so little resources. But, it looked like they were upholding the treaty. I'll plot spoil enough to say that I later learned the only real breach in treaty was the stormers did comondeer one ambulance for those that they had pulled out.

It was horrible. Blood, fire, smoke death, gore. Everywhere. Is this simply what a battle is? I could smell it, I could smell charred flesh even. The station, previously the central station. Was engulfed in fire. Even if it hadn't been the sight of such death. It probably would still have to be torn down. I doubted firefighters had even gone into it. Fine by me. The amount of smoke being produced was truly unreal. The accelerant used, does not go out. At least not like that. They were especially told to use this combination of two commonplace things, and for that very reason. And for the reader's sake. I will not interrupt the most dramatic part to explain the physics of it. However, I will take the time in the appendix for those interested. But, there, everything was on fire. So much accelerant, so much fire. But also still a sprinkler system. But, have you ever tried putting out a campfire? Blowing out a candle. Noticed how much it smoke it produces then? Same effect. Enough so that my mother insisted on putting the lid on the candle right at that moment. It was a massive smoke plume. Showing this battlefield, for a great distance.

I simply couldn't believe what I was seeing. I disconnected, rejecting, if you will, my surroundings. Then I looked down. There was a little girl. She looked like my sister. A lot like my sister, even was dressed like her. I was sure it wasn't her. But it sure scared me. She was one of the youngest there. Was she the youngest victim?

We weren't there for long. One of only a handful of times in my career that we received a call in person. And the boss was told by the Fire Chief personally. We rode there quickly. The destination was not far away. All the while I wondered. What could be so horrible for us to leave that? They didn't have anywhere near enough personnel as it was. And surely more firefighters were coming in from everywhere. I wondered how hospitals would handle it. It was so severe, they couldn't just go in drive by, could they? Like most any place. There were only so many hospitals, so many beds.

We were briefed on the way there. If I hadn't just seen what I had just seen. Even I wouldn't have believed it. On the way, the rain was beginning to pick up. Perhaps rain adhering to smoke spores, making it rain. No, that just makes fog. Well, we didn't care anyways. I began to see some smoke. It was a juvenile correction facility. Baby jail. Kiddie jail. Whatever you want to call it. It hits an alarm in my soul whenever anyone says it.

I saw the driver, and he was going over 60, nearly top speed. We slammed through the gate, into the jail. And it was a sliding / retracting fence type gate at that. No one came out to us, no one tried to stand in our way, and block us from getting in. Which was for the best. The engineer, while I doubt he would have aimed for them. He certainly wouldn't have stopped. He would have just run them over. Probably wouldn't have even flinched. He never said so. He didn't have to. Something about him, no, everything about him, shouted it. Screamed it.

The first thing we did was we got in. Though far from procedure, I was actually surprised that we didn't drive the fire truck clean into the jail to get in. We worked quick. I suppose we were a well-oiled machine. As I have said. With our equipment. We can get into pretty much anything. So getting in was not the hard part. No, that was easy. It was getting out that was hard. No, we were never trapped. What we opened we opened and left open. It was rescue.

Once we got inside. We all realized the true magnitude of what had happened. There was smoke everywhere. And they were in their cells. Some shouting out for help, some slumped and out, a few simply quiet. The place had abandoned. At least the guards were gone. But most assuredly, it was not abandoned. Naturally we rushed to get them out. We didn't know where the fire was, which only added to things. Obviously we rushed to save them. Initially we grabbed two and rushed them outside. Then just outside. We met the warden. Where that (expletive) (expletive) had been all this time, I still to this day do not know. We confronted him, or perhaps he confronted us would be more appropriate. I apologize that I cannot recall conversations word for word. But I remember generally what happened. I remember he was in a panic. Basically trying to get us to hurry put out the fire. Deal was. It was an older prison. And originally it hadn't been for juvenile delinquents. It had been the main prison for the area. But, populations grew and so did Madison. We needed a new, larger prison. And this old one was made into something for underage convicts (and those underage denied bail I might add). But, when it was first designed, they also put in a basement. Most buildings in the heartland / heart of fly-over-country have to have one because of the tornado threat. It's not as bad as in Kansas, but still a threat. And the basement of the jail. Through intended to be a tornado shelter. It was used by the corrections department as a mechanic's shop for all the corrections' department's vehicles. And while for the most part the department of corrections outgrew the jail. The mechanic's shop it maintained and even had it come to fill the entire basement. And it was in that mechanic's shop that the fire started. I didn't know how. I'm sure we brought in an arson investigator. But, I didn't hang around to find out. Most any mechanic's shop will have motor oil and other such flammables. So it's not so shocking that you could have a dangerous fire in one. Bu this fire. It was, of itself, self-contained within the basement / mechanic's shop. But it did spread within the service bay. Also like most any mechanic's shop it also had a goodly amount of tires kept on hand. Now, when most people think of tires burning, they probably think of Cajuns burning tires to pass a good time. But, it's actually quite serious. Enough so that tires are not allowed in generic landfills. They are required to go into special tire / rubber landfills. And if one manages to catch on fire, it can burn for weeks or months. And this place had a good supply of tires.

We took the time to deal with him at all because he knew things. And he knew how to open the cells. We could get in without him. But as you have seen; we couldn't get in as fast. There was some back and forth. But not much. Wasn't time for much. Deal was, with what had gone on in downtown earlier that day. They knew they couldn't hold them in. There was some suspicion as well that it was linked to that. But, the same day as the Boston Marathon Bombings. They first thought that there had been a 3rd bomb at the Kennedy presidential library in another part of the same city. Wrong. Was a coincidental explosion caused by a coincidental fire. He wouldn't talk. We didn't have time to talk much to him. One of us shouted out that we should kill him. Wasn't me. I can tell you that whoever it was, was serious. But the boss said no. He knows things. And dead men tell no access codes. We need him to open up all the doors. As I have said, err, dictated, he wouldn't. But, we had means to make him talk. We pulled his

(insert mule picture here)
Houston•Barrow•San Francisco•Upstate New York•Boca Raton

pants down and stuck the Jaws of Life in between his butt cheeks. Then, when the boss realized that that in and of itself wasn't enough. He made the decision to go ahead, and separate his hips with the Jaws of Life. The warden screamed out in pure agony. We could all hear the sounds of his bones, well, I hesitate to say breaking. But certainly was not mere joints popping. The boss seemed bothered. But I would be lying if I said that that I was not glad to hear it. How he was able to remain conscious, I have no idea. But that was enough. And he was able to tell us how to get into controls (which the getting into part was not essential for us, but there was the issue of how long would it take) and then open up all the doors. Out of fear of him lying, we kept him conscious, just in case we needed him for some purpose.

Then in we went. We never even bothered to go down into the service bay. Why? Probably wasn't anyone down there. (and between you me and the preverbal fence post. If there was, probably they would have had something to do with it anyway.) And like in the main emergency. Just so many wounded, so few resources. Same reason that they didn't even bother going up in to the adjacent buildings. Focus in the highest concentration. Also as I have discussed. We knew there to be dangerous flammable chemicals. Who knew what they'd do. What we did do was to try to quarantine the service bay. And give the smoke some escape other than the interior of the prison. Like I dictated; the fire itself seemed contained in the mechanic's shop. So we did something unheard-of in firefighting. We split up. This. You do not train for this. No one does. It is beyond the pale, it is over-the-top. Some could get out on their own. A few even helped others out. But, most needed us to take them out. Also under any remotely normal situation. They would be treated for smoke inihation. But we weren't anywhere near remotely capable in terms of both manpower and supplies. We merely hoped getting into the fresh air would be enough. That's certainly the first thing to do in carbon monoxide, get outside and clear your lungs. We were simply trying to get them out as fast as possible. And I was certainly no exception. It all was so surreal. There's a lot of things that I could have expected. Would have expected. Dictatorially powerful jailors and warden. Ignoring and allowing whatever violence and danger. These I wouldn't even be surprised by. But this, even I would have called preposterous, and anti-police rhetoric. But, I was there. It was real. But, I worked through it, I did what needed to be done. For obvious reasons we worked quick. We didn't even bother trying to call for backup. A co-firefighter, without permission but with informing us, took inmates into the office for them to call for help. We did run out of air on the tanks. We just did.

A few random people came out. It was also, on top of everything else, cold. For the time of year it was relatively warm. But, it was cold. A few brought out blankets and towels as blankets. One old lady brought out her oxygen tanks as a makeshift treatment. Not many people came out at all, at least for what this was. But there were those that did. A few. What most did was they hauled off as many as they could to a nearby hospital. And as I predicted, the obvious filled the hospitals. The majority of those that came out, only showed up once. I don't know who was taken where. But it was obvious it was going to be a real drive to reach a hospital that was open. We hauled out the bodies of teenagers we knew would not come around. We tried to give those that had a chance to live some priority. On two different occasions we did what we could to keep them from going back in. All the while the rain had been picking up. Threw it all I wondered if I was in shock.

It was hours before we had completely cleared the place. Often in firefighting, you're really operating on fumes, on force. You just make yourself go once you're in there. That was beyond anything. Our tanks were only approved for 25 minutes; we couldn't just re-fill them. It's compressed air; but the compression system is as the firehouse. And even at that it takes time. But somehow we went on. I don't know how. And even after all that. We still had the gruesome task of declared the dead to have died one-by-one. Eventually, we were simply waiting for the coroner to show up.

"How many do you think died?" I asked.

"Well, counting those that got to a hospital, or at least were taken to one. Probably more than half," said the boss.

"No, no, I mean-" I said.

"In the thing, that we left" he said.

"Yeah," I said.

"Well, I don't know," he said.

"1/3," (pause) "HALF!-" I said.

"Lost 2/3rd's when they stormed Normandy beach," she said.

"What-" I said.

"Yeah," she said.

"According to this," I said doing research in my phone, "There was this one guy, calling him the angel of the storm-"

"This storm's letting up, for the time of year. Pretty warm," said the boss.

"No, no, I think 'The Storm at Madison' is what they're going to call it," I said.

"No, there was this one guy, a veteran in uniform actually. Calling him the angel of the storm. He had a gun, was shooting through the police blockade, now among the dead," I said.

"How on earth can you shoot through that much bulletproof-" he said.

"He had a gun from first used in WWII as anti-tank defense. It can shoot through whatever it jolly well pleases," I said.

"Been found a group of other traders like that with similar weapons," said the boss.

"Hey, if they hadn't been stopped, probably would have been a lot less deaths. Lot less children would have died," I paused and said, "Might have been even less officers killed."

"How they could prosecute this-" he said.

"From what I'm hearing. They might instead prosecute the officers for having not surrendered." he said.

The boss was shocked. "-"

Before he could speak. I said "Come on. You saw the bodies. The destruction-"

"Well in that case, so did you. What happened. That was a punishment-"

"Never say never, according to this article on (news source) the high ranking officers. They locked themselves in a safe room, at lease most of them did." he said.

"You mean. They sent their supervisees in to die. And the cohorsers, they just stayed safe and sound-" I said.

"Never say never," she said, looking at something "Can't trust everything you read on the internet."

"And, and after all they've done. And all they've put in policy and ordered to be done. And life just goes on! And that's that!" I said horrified.

"Actually, according to this. They could have gassed them. Their shelter was not air tight. But, they didn't want to be seen as war criminals-" he said.

"WHAT! Just, just as a matter of what they come across as-" I said.

"Oh, you know it's a war crime to gas people. Furthermore. Wasn't even needful. Already had those girls. Those surviving were just trying to get out of there," he said.

"Well would it make you feel better if they were impaled with bayonets?!" I said.

"According to this, was one room where the officers were so well armed. And had so much body armor. Had to turn the place inferno to defeat the police." she said.

"Sounds like the whole battle to me," I said.

"About what you said, about the piles of bodies," said the boss.

"Yes?" I said.

"Actually, a lot of them. They just brought up gang members from Chicago-" he said.

"First of all. Believe me. They weren't all. Second, growing up in a dangerous area. Being in a street gang. Face it. Violence is new to what's going on. Probably just better fighters," I said, "Man it is cold!"

"Well if you hadn't taken off your shirt-" said the boss.

"Well, I wanted something to cover them other than prison jump- FINALLY!" I sorta-shouted.

"What?!" said the boss.

"A journalist! Finally!" I said.

(insert mule picture here)
Houston•Barrow•San Francisco•Upstate New York•Boca Raton

I went over. I think my coerts followed. Then I saw one of them. One of the bodies. One I had neither pulled out nor declared dead. He looked young, even for underage. Possibly the youngest here, certainly one of them. And he was naked. I thought "GOD! Sexual abuse!" I lost it. I saw the journalist with a camera. I picked him up, and ran over to the journalist. I screamed. "Look what you did!!..." After that I continued screaming. Don't know what. Don't remember. I remember the general idea. But, you can guess what sort of things would be screamed.

Then my boss arrived. "HEY! Put Him Down!" he screamed at me. "You Wana Get Fired?!"

"What! What Are You Gunu Do About It!? You Gunu Fire Me!" We were both not doing ok. After what we had been through. And, I guess he saw that in me. The look, I never myself saw it. But, he saw me. Looking at him like that. Daring him. Daring him to fire me.

"*We're all mad here*" – Alice through the Looking Glass by Charles Ludwig Dogerson A.K.A. Lewis Carol

Chapter Five

For all people thought, of all that had gone on, all that led up to it. Thinking Madison was the epi-center of all of it. Eye of the storm would probably be more accurate. While the nation was holding its breath like Fort Sumter meets the Cuban Missile crisis. For all people thought that the governor was scared into making peace and pardoning everyone (literally everyone). The truth is, not really so. The battle, the storm happened. And it was horrible. The rains combined with the blood was so horrible city sewer workers were forced out of where they had been working unrelated by the smell of blood. But, after it, it was over. The police (those who were left) went home. No one was out. And if in any of the other possible sites, if it had gone sideways in Houston, or Los Angelous, or Baltimore. Well then. That would have been that for the rest of the country. But not us. We had already had ours. It was over. Even the police went home. Perhaps we truly were 77 square miles surrounded by reality, but maybe not. Enough so that my former (will explain) superior told me probably the only police involvement whatsoever was two officers clearing a parking garage after one of the planes hit it. And I replied, "yes, imagine that. A hero. For disobeying orders." It really was a calm night. I wouldn't say tranquil. But calm, Except of course for the families of course. But, not for all. Their never truly were 0 police out on regular duties, but it was pretty close. It actually began before it began. Simply when the cat's away the mice will play. Police reallocated resources, and criminals took advantage. After the fact (and even some while it was still going on); it got worse. Enough so there were random people picking up the slack. Even rumors of those just back from you-know-what answering calls for the police. The fires of themselves from the battle also proved to be a formidable foe. At first they could not be fought at all. They were just desperately trying to save the injured. Law enforcement had been brought in, nearly pushed it nationally over the edge almost bringing in Marshall law and enough National Guardsmen to carry it out. But, not really much of any additional firefighters. Sure when calls went out. There were volunteer firefighters and paramedics that came in from rural areas. Ones that usually we (and those I worked with and myself especially) were instead support for. But, for the most part. Not much additional EMS personal were brought in. By the time those that weren't defiantly dead were taken care of. It was out of control. Who knows how long the central precinct alone burned? Obviously there was fire crews on site. But not me. No, I had to get out of there. I had simply seen too much

(insert fire and flames here)

Then I saw in my dream that when they were got out of the wilderness, the presently saw a state before them, and the name of that state was Florida; and at the state there is a city kept called Boca Raton. It is kept all year long. It beareth the name of Boca Raton because the state where it is kept is crazier than a bedbug; and also, because all that is sold, or cometh thither, is elderly. As is the saying of the wise "All that cometh is vanity."

This town is no new-erected place, but a thing that standuth since 1895; I will show you the origin of it.

Almost five thousand years agone there were pilgrims walking to the Celestial City, as these two honest persons are; and Addison Mizner, Henry Flagler, and Bernard Romans, with their companions, perceiving by the path that the pilgrims made that their way into the city lay through this town of Florida, they contrived here to set up a resort, a resort wherein should be sold all sorts of elderly, and that it should last all the year long. Therefore at this resort are all such merchandise sold, as adult diapers, walkers, artificial hips, hearing aids, dentures, portable oxygen, medical compression socks, elevators, nursing care, condos, medicine, motorized wheelchairs, and delights of all sorts, as wrinkle cream, liver spot cream, bingo, soft food, large print, wigs, arthritis

(insert mule picture here)

Houston•Barrow•San Francisco•Upstate New York•Boca Raton

cream, very early dinners, food thickener, speaking up, magnifiers, sugar free candy, cafeterias, grandkids, Polident, and what not

(insert fire and flames here)

Ah Florida. Where the men dial 911 to brag about their muscles. The women stay with their husbands even after they learn their also their grandfather. And the 12 year old girls get tried as adults for pinching a boys butt; even if he liked and wanted her to do it again. All these things actually happened. My first sign I was in Florida was that I was exchanging between freeways, and I was on one of those extremely high overpass curves (you know the type) and low and behold. The woman in front of me was yaking on the mobile phone, while applying mascara and smoking. It's worth noting that she was not a 6 armed Indian Goddess. I remember thinking to myself that if she would only put the cigarette in one side of her mouth and have the phone supported by the shoulder on the other side. Then she could brush her hair while she was at it. Ok I lied. I really was thinking that if she made anything of a routine of that she wouldn't be around much longer. All the while keeping my distance from her of course. For those of you my readers that will wonder how. She had the telephone and cigarette in one hand; and with the other she was putting on makeup. I assume she was driving with her knee; though this was Florida. So no telling.

Boca Raton. It's a major city. Not really an international city. Not as well-known as say, Chicago, or New York. But, most anyone most anywhere in America would at least recognize the name, and at least have a general idea where it is. Like Napa Valley or Berkley, we live in the shadow of a larger city. In their case it's San Francisco; in ours it's Miami. And in both cases closer (smaller) cities and towns to exist. Like the

(insert mule picture here)

Metroplex we have major cities close enough for people to regularly commute back and forth from one to the other (or vice-a-versa). Not like Minneapolis and St. Paul close. But close enough. Like Los Angelous, the majority of people living in the city do not live within the proper city limits.

Ah Boca Raton. The world headquarters of Office Depot, and True Green Enterprises, and The Bridge Group. (Would you believe I only know what one of those things are?) I was glad to be here. Especially after the long drive all the way from southern Wisconsin (or as my new co-workers came to call it constipationborough.) I decided to drive here because I hate flying, no I hate airport security; also the easiest way to get my car across several states. They claim that as part of it. You give up your rights. Pah! I say that's a load of Politician. I'm sure the security checks go over real well with that firefighter's victims. And the pointless rules about carry on! I remember a story about a Soviet boy crying upset over having had their stuff inspected; and his mother reassuring him saying how they were going to America. Where that could never happen. But I digress. There were perks of living in Boca Raton instead of Madison. For starters having to drive only 20 miles down to Sawgrass Mills in Sunrise to get to a Books-A-Million instead of 30 miles to Janesville. Of course for more in-town there's always Bookwise. But that's not the only one. Also there's not freezing your tuchis off every winter. Goodbye Snowplow! Hello 11 months of air conditioning.

(insert fire and flames here)

"Welcome to your first day with the Boca Raton Fire Department,"

"It's good to be here," I said.

"So, where did you come from?" I was asked.

"Madison," I said.

"Madison?"

"Yes, Madison Wisconsin," I said.

"Wait, that means, that you were, were, you were there-"

"Well, I saw it, but, no, err, not exactly," I said.

"What, what, what do you mean?"

"What was it like?"

"Well, I remember it was cold, but for the time of year and the climate. It was warm. Quite warm. After it happened, a thunderstorm moved in off Lake Michigan," I said, "I wasn't there right when it all went down. But I did see it in the brunt of EMS response. It was horrific. For all the claims I have faced of being some sort of sympathizer, or reveling in it. The truth is that I wasn't happy. I certainly wasn't calling for violence or uprisings. My superior feared that stuff like this and unrest. Would lead to anarchy. Well, I wasn't fearful of that. Didn't seem plausible that in this day in time we could have true anarchy. But what did seem plausible is we would be destabilized. Revolutions, we being Americans wouldn't understand this, but revolution doesn't mean things are going to get better. In fact they almost never do. What I feared was some dictator would crawl out from under some rock, and a banana republic would form (and I do not mean the store) and they we'd have tyranny by decree, like a king. Because, ultimately it's a vigilante force. It's run by people. People are most assuredly not perfect. Even when we have the rule of law. Ruled by laws not monarchs, they get around it by making it so complicated it could not be understood. It originally was such that everything had to be clearly and plainly spelled out in black and white for everyone to understand. But between that and other factors, getting around the laws. And making laws that violate the law that regulate the laws (that is the constitution). Well, that's why I won't fly. They say the law says X, but in reality the law is in violation of the law. But where was I going with this? Oh yes! Point is, look at other parts of the world. We may have problems. Laws that are unfair and illegal. Loopholes, and more grievances still; but it can get worse. It can get much worse. That's why what happened there, why revolution. It should be held off as a last resort. But, that's what they did. They did all they could to overwhelm things by peaceful means. But, those girls were suffering RIGHT NOW err THEN. And however long overwhelming took; that's how long they'd continue to go through what they went through," I said, "I think I may have gone off on a tangent."

"Ya think! But, were you really, err, was, was the response as overwhelmed as they portrayed on the news?"

"Possibly moreso. But, I wouldn't know. I saw it. But I never was actually a responder to it." I said.

"But, I would have figured that something like that, every ambulance and fire engine in town would be there, In 9/11 every available and off duty firefighter was called into duty."

"Every fire apparatus near town was brought in. Except one. One fire engine did not. I was on that fire engine," I said.

"What? What do you mean-"

"There was a fire. It was in juvenile lockup, err, technically in the basement. We were just trying to get them out," I said.

"What? What are you talking about?"

"No, no, I think I remember this."

"Yeah, the fire itself we never battled. Frankly it could all burn down for all we cared. Though I was there late into the night and well into the wee hours of the morning. It didn't. Deal was the basement was an auto shop by and for the prison system. There was all that you would expect in most any auto shop. Including tires-"

Then they all got it.

"Yeah, MFD didn't have the equipment to blow the smoke out of a large building. Thought I'm pretty sure they're now getting such a fan," I said.

"Couldn't the apparatus be brought up from Chicago?"

"Well that depends on what you're definition of 'could' is. If by could you mean 'could it be moved from the City of the Broad Shoulders to the State Capitol of Wisconsin?' then your answer would be yes. It was physically possible for such apparatus to be moved to the underage prison. If by could you mean 'could the blower apparatus be moved to the fire soasto save the lives of those trapped, or at least unconscious within' then the answer would be 'no.' We waited for the coroner to collect the body for hours. We were expecting the medical examiner to arrive from Milwaukee. But, instead it was from Chicago. Were examiners from Milwaukee, and all throughout Wisconsin and even adjacent areas. But most went to the obvious. We waited for hours and hours after we called. Sure firefighters, lights and sirens blaring, I'm sure they would have a faster response time. But still. It's a ways off. It was a real 'why bother?' Only reason any survived was that we got them out. And like at the storm, we were horribly overwhelmed and unequipped. Both in manpower and equipment. And even at that a horrific number died. And moreso still I know got to a hospital (or at least they tried to take them) but still they didn't pull through.

"Just, umm-"

"Just how horrific was it?"

"Horrific, all throughout it I felt like I walking through a Nazi holocaust gas chamber. So surreal-" I said, "I-I, do you mind? I don't like to talk about this."

"Oops."

"Our bad."

"So, like, is it true that you have a lot of good cheese up there in Wisconsin?"

"Is it true that you have a lot of old people here in Boca Raton?" I asked.

"Oh, is that a bigoted perception?"

I chuckled and said "No, but like, like you said, do you have a lot of old people?"

And then one steyotype / cliché that was accurate then came to be. I was pouring a cup of coffee at that moment when it came in. We've all seen it on TV. The alarm blares, everyone in the fire station freezes up to listen to what the emergency is. Well, that's one thing wherein Hollywood hasn't Hollywooded it up. For obvious reasons, it is important to hear the call come in. And we really do have poles to slide down in an emergency. We rush out in an emergency. So yes, we really do freeze up when a call comes in. But, like I said, I just so happened to be pouring a cup of coffee when the call came in. Now, couldn't just completely freeze up, that's obvious. So, I quickly stopped pouring. And I was paying more attention to the obvious, so I didn't even pay attention

as I stopped pouring. And the coffee was really hot, so. I burned myself. And then had
to suppress an "ouch." Didn't do a very good job of it.

(insert fire and flames here)

At first we didn't realize the severity of it. We knew it was bad. We knew there might
be fatalities. But we didn't realize just how bad it truly was. We arrived in 6 minutes 40
seconds. Right at the average response time for BRFD. A car had driven off the road.
It was after rush hour. Probably stopped off for some drinks, then headed back home to
Royal Palm Yacht and Country Club. A gated community; and as the name implies,
VERY expensive. But, there is an old story about death. I wish that I knew what it was,
but I remember there was some part wherein some rich old lady tried to bribe the grim
reaper. Well, let's just say death wasn't on the take. Same here. We assumed him to
be ETOH (basically firefighter slang for drunk). Definatly it was a vehicle fire. But it was
not a normal vehicle fire. Oh no, far from it. He had gone off a residential street and
crashed directly into a gas main. I do not mean like one of those little ones, like maybe
a house's gas meter. Or anything like that. I mean the kind that surface over
waterways and the gas company puts fence-like stuff on it to keep it from being used as
a bridge. It was so bad that there was no point even if it had been possible to even try a
vehicle and machinery rescue. Even if it had been possible. Which it wasn't. It was
way too hot. The moment I opened the door of the pumper truck, even before I stepped
out. I could feel the intense heat of the massive inferno. I mentioned how long it took
because in that time the car (and everything and everyone in it) had been completely
incinerated. But there was an adjacent mansion. Already calls had gone out to Florida
Public utilities but, until they shut off the gas. Wasn't much we could do. Like I said,
much. There was some containment. A tree was near it, or more specifically, near the

(insert mule picture here)

house. It wasn't actually near enough to be directly lit on fire. Rather there was so much heat coming off the collision; or more accurately perhaps the gas-main-turned-flame-thrower-/-blow-torch that the ironwood had simply burst into flames on its own. And it was well advanced in terms of that. There was nothing to be done for the car. In fact we already knew we wouldn't find bodies. They would have already been incinerated. We rushed to cool the tree and the house.

We saw that the family had already gotten outside. They assured us that they had all gotten out ok. That was good, it was a big house.

We sprayed the ironwood and then took it down and away like a wildfire crew. There wasn't much else to remove, Even the grass seemed incinerated and the loam and Boca fine sand baked. The heat was so intense there was nothing left.

(insert fire and flames here)

It didn't take too long for the gas line to be turned off. Officially we were on re-flash watch. But there wasn't too much point. All that there was that could have burned already had. Even if they had turned the gas back on, still wouldn't have been anything we could have done. Would have just poured out until it was ignited and exploded.

Police arrived almost immediately after the gas went off.

"Panoz! What's a Panoz!" shouted the officer.

"A what?" said my boss.

"Ran the license plate through, still had the impression of the letters and numbers even if the rear plate's paint burned off," said the officer.

(insert mule picture here)

"Oh, that's an extremely expensive brand of car. They're made up in Georgia, to give you an idea how expensive, they have not made 700 cars, and they've been around since the late 80's. This is said to be the most expensive gated neighborhood in the country. So, guess this is the place to find something like that," I said.

"Well, I found the owner's name, address is real close to here," said the officer.

"Guess our theory was right," said the boss.

"Rich drunk on the way home?" said the officer.

"Yup,"

"Sorry your first job with us had a Death on Scene,"

"Job?" I said.

"What? I'm from New York. Came here because was a small new England town. Wasn't any career positions."

"Oh, may be more than one. Police will have to determine who goes missing. Can't even find a body," I said.

"Yes, I know," came the solemn reply.

"Oh, was mild compared to my first, as you put it, 'Job,'" I said.

"Oh. What happened?"

"It was awful. We weren't the first there. They had already sprayed pencil streams in through holes, to cool it down enough that we could get in at all. It was a big house, and all modern construction. Everything was flammable, everything was on fire. It was a stupid accident that caused it. We found that," I paused and said, "Buncha kids were having a sleepover. Smoke took all of them out. Counselors were sent out to the firehouse ex-post-facto to make sure we were all ok. I-I-I don't like to talk about it. Could we change the subject?"

"So, like, As we asked earlier, do you really have a lot of good cheese in Wisconsin?" I was asked.

"Meh, I'm just as content with the selection at Publix," I said.

"Lactose intolerant?" I was asked.

"No! I mean, does everybody in Seattle, Washington drink coffee every-" I said.

"Everybody outside of Seattle does, except maybe in Utah."

"Eh, fair point," I said.

"How you holding up?" I was asked.

"Oh, glad to be out of there. I know it's passed, and all, but,-" I said.

"Now you have a new gig here in Boca Raton."

"Yeah, just, just, the things I saw. So extreme. Who deals with that level of- Well, it may be over, but regardless. I'm out, I got away."

I saw the look on the face of a paramedic that had obviously and clearly overheard.

"What?" I said concerned, "What?! Somebody! Please! Tell me!"

Another paramedic walked over and said "It was a few weeks back. We here got a call. From a nursing home," he said.

"A nursing home? In Florida? How bizarre," I said sarcastically. I knew there had not been a nursing home fire, err, at the very least. I knew of no nursing home fire.

"They had served fruit cocktail. From. A. Can."

I cocked my head to one side like dogs do when they are confused.

"Well, they, naturally, used those commercial sized giganto-normous cans, and, for whatever the reason, they must have mixed them. Well, one of them was contaminated, apparently." he said.

"You mean, like, botulism?" I said.

He nodded.

"But, but, you responded. They figured it out. Surely it-"

"Well, there were those that could take nothing by mouth. Those that weren't willing to eat it. But, what you must keep in mind is. This was a nursing home; and botulism is about as bad as it gets to begin with," he said.

"But, well, I mean-"

The first paramedic said to me, "There was one that wasn't even a resident. Simply had lunch there as part of visiting a relative. They often offer such services. Even got 2 workers who were stealing food, as opposed to packing a lunch."

Chapter Six

Like I had said. I was glad to be out. And, as you would expect, that story about the nursing home did, well, but that's that. Like also I said, it may have been over, but still I was glad to be out. I had found peace, peace in the Head of the Rat.

(insert fire and flames here)

Henrietta B. was not a young woman. But most assuredly she was not a woman whose age had surpassed her weight. "I Can Take Care of Myself!" That was her catchphrase.

Travax was a young poor kid. Most assuredly he was not perfect; but same goes for everyone else on the face of the planet. His family couldn't afford much. Who knows? Maybe it truly wasn't fair what he had. Maybe he truly was just keeping up with the Joneses. The discussion of that issue is not the purpose of this book. But one thing is for sure. His embarrassment was real.

"HEYY! Do Not Grab My Purse!" she shouted. He had tried to grab her purse and run. But she was stronger than she looked. It was like trying to turn a key, but the lock sticks and it just ends up hurting your thumb because it won't budge. Travax didn't actually fall. But he did stumble.

"I didn't mean to!" he lied.

"Yeah, like Mr. Nixon didn't mean to erase 18 minutes of tape. You're coming with me," she said, grabbing him and dragging him off.

(insert fire and flames here)

It had been a quiet day at the firehouse. Early in my shift we had responded to two false alarms at Tucci's Fire N Coal Pizza and at Mizner Pizzeria; guess it was just a bad day for pizza. But those were merely goofs. No fire, no nothing. Basically a calm day. To some it might be called boring. But, just as there is a Chinese blessing / curse "May you like an interesting life" so boring was good. It is in a tranquil garden that nothing happens. Maybe a cherry blossom falls from the tree into a pond. Maybe a little splash from a coy fish. Not much. It's not an action movie which there is lots of things blowing up, bullets going everywhere. One makes a good story; the other makes a good reality.

(insert fire and flames here)

Henrietta B. arrived at her Pearl City home. Her Grandfather had been one of the first to move in back in the teens. The house had been in her family ever since.

For all that everyone thought that Travax was in a gang. It wasn't true. That's not to say that paths had never crossed; but he was not a gang member. He was years away from even being a teenager. He wasn't in single digits. But he was not a teenager.

"Now Go Clean Yourself Up!" she told him.

He was both relieved and worried. He was very glad not to be turned into police. But? What was happening? What was this? What was about to happen?

(insert fire and flames here)

"Hello, I haven't met you here before," I said.

"That's because you've been here 3 days," said the paramedic.

"Well, this is your fire barn too?" I said.

"Barn?" he said.

"What, my last station was the farthest out station the department had. As much as anything we were mutual support for rural and volunteer departments," I said.

"Where was that?" he asked.

"Madison Wisconsin," I said, fearing having to re-tell my story.

"OH! You're that guy," he said.

"I, I am?" I said.

"Everyone in BRFD knows we now have a transplant from that," he said.

"Oh, well, that's shouldn't surprise me," I said.

"You know, I've seen a good bit in my time too," he said.

"How long have you been here?" I asked

"Few weeks," he said.

"You a transfer in too?" I said.

"Yeah," he replied.

"Were-from?" I said.

"Around really," he said, "Started out with Houston FD. And, teenage boy tries to jump from a moving car. Parents were parents. Couldn't let him jump out; certainly not onto a freeway. So they grabbed him, he wouldn't get back in, he was dragged to death. Little girl crushed to death by bookcase. But, there was some REALLY bad stuff going on down in Space City, let me tell you. And not all of it was even stuff I came across in my line of work. My mother worked as a school counselor. And she and I are of very different mindsets. Nevertheless. She worked in the part that wasn't even 'officially', emphasis on my air-quotes, a punishment part of the alternative school. But even she admitted that had been told not to come in when they were checking the kids in. That she didn't want to see how they were treated, that it would just distress her. Not word for word. But, Soon as I got my green card, I was outa there. After that I had to get away. I eventually found a position in San Francisco Fire department. For a while, I had gotten away. Found peace. It may have been the job was simply too much-"

"For me, I had to get away. IT may have come to an end. But, still, I am free. I have gotten away," I said.

"Well, for me, for a time, that probably was my experience. I was happy walking up the steep hills of San Francisco. But, eventually, I guess IT caught up with me," he said.

Cautiously I asked, "What happened?"

"Mass. Teen. Suicide."

That took me by surprise. After a moment I asked, "I think I remember hearing a news blurb about that. Was it as terrible as, as it seemed?"

He scoffed as he said "News Blurb!" Then he said "Well, If by terrible you mean like a deadly car accident that makes 10's of thousands of people late to work and stops up the highway for everybody making a big headache. Or do you mean terrible as in a horrifying tragedy?"

"I-I I'm sorry," I said.

"I'm sorry. I didn't mean to do off on you like that. Deal is. What's really bothering me, this, err, that. It's the tip of the iceberg, compared to all teen sufferings. So much, high school is hell. And they're problems, they're called drama queens, well, you get the point. After that one, I didn't run off as fast as I could. Houston, I was so bad if immigration hadn't gone through much sooner. If I had had to stay and wait, well. I was about to go back to the old country, but, there it was, well," he said.

"Well, Houston and San Francisco are certainly two different cities," I said.

"Yeah, no kidding. And just to make it interesting, there's Austin-"

(insert fire and flames here)

Travax went into the restroom. He didn't know that he was in that much danger, but he certainly was in that much trouble. He climbed up on the toilet, maybe he could go out the window? No, he tried. It was hard to open, and he was afraid of the noise.

Then he noticed it. An old gas heater. He had once seen in a movie where a captive turned on the water, found an abandoned air vent under tile, and managed to get water pouring into the vent. That way someone would come, someone would begin to catch on. Being a kid (although a delinquent) he thought that if he opened up the gas line then someone would realize something was wrong. And come check it out.

He turned on the gas, although he didn't know it, it hadn't been used for decades. So it was very stuck. But, he muscled it open. There had been a good chance that after all that time, the gas lines would have clogged. Well, partially they had. It slowed considerably the amount that came out. But, he could hear it quietly hissing out. And quietly enough that the old hag-bag wouldn't hear it! He felt it. "*No*" he thought to

(insert mule picture here)
Houston•Barrow•San Francisco•Upstate New York•Boca Raton

himself "*It's defiantly not simply heating as it's meant to, no heat, no flame, no furnace going.*" SUCCESS!

"*PU! Gas stinks!*"

(insert fire and flames here)

Henrietta B. had just opened the can and put it into the pot. Like most older people, she was herself not that hard-of-hearing. But she was hard-of-smelling. As a by-product she would over-salt her food. She put the pot on the NXR stove. She went to get out bowls. She decided to use the brand new ones from K-mart. After all, technically he was company.

"*Oops.*" She realized she forgot to turn the stove on.

(insert fire and flames here)

That Austin thought would have to hold. We got a call. It was presumed to be a FGI (Fire Gas Ignition). Like with most house fires, most all calls actually. We scrambled to the pumper truck. As you may know, we even leave the turnout gear pants on the floor in such a way that we only have to step into them. (Take that little miss "clean up your room!" You know who you are.) And like that we were blazing away down the street.

(insert fire and flames here)

Travax was trapped and powerless. What was where?!!? What had just happened. Automatically he started to scream. In panic? Or in pain? It was everywhere! It was everything! Even his lungs! HE COULDN'T BREATHE!!

(insert fire and flames here)

Quickly Henrietta B. grabbed the sink sprayer. Her Dress Was On Fire. She rushed to put it out. Grateful for a sink sprayer. It was going out. She could fell the flames! It hurt! But, in it all, she was grateful to have the sprayer. She shouted to keep away from the fire. She rushed to put out the source. Then the magnitude of it hit her. Her home was on fire. It was everywhere. It took her a moment to realize the danger! This had passed something merely bursting, or an incipient stage fire.

Her grandkids had just dropped off their little kid with her, again. What was she?! La Petite Academy.

She rushed past her beloved table and tablecloth, now going up in flames, she rushed to beat out his clothes. He screamed. She then grabbed his hand as much as just grabbed him and rushed out the front door.

She screamed for help. Someone simply had to come out, to help. "*That Other Boy! He's Still In There!*" She thought.

Then she heard it. Her oxygen tanks. Most of the time she didn't use them. But, she heard them. It was exploding!

(insert fire and flames here)

(insert mule picture here)
Houston•Barrow•San Francisco•Upstate New York•Boca Raton

When we arrived we were not the first ones there. But it was so close that they hadn't even charged their hoses yet. The main attraction was a large, mean, old woman who was going crazy on the front lawn. They were trying to calm her down.

"There's a kid in there!" someone shouted.

"*Guess that's what she was trying to say*," I thought.

We rushed in. In this case, I strictly mean "we" in the general plural sense. As part of two-in-two-out I and another stood guard outside in case the two firefighters going in needed themselves to be rescued

(insert fire and flames here)

"How you holding up?" asked the earlier paramedic.

"Eh, pretty well. And you?" I said.

"Oh, Ok, We got him to the hospital," he said.

"Oh! So he survived," I said.

"Nope," he said.

"Eyaie!" I said.

"Sorry to break the news. Shiesh, you've been with us 3 days and already we've responded to 2 fatalities, both involving fire, I'm sorry to be such a poor welcome sport," he said.

(insert mule picture here)

"Meh, it's ok. Nothing could ever compare to what I saw in the storm," I said, "Err, at least," I fake spit "twoo twoo. I sure hope to God nothing ever could."

"Yeah, I'm holding up pretty well, at least considering," he said.

"That's good," I said.

"BRPD just hauled the homeowner off," he said.

"What? What for exactly?" I said.

"Not sure, but. That thing with that boy was fishy as possible," he said.

"How exactly?" I said.

"Well, when social services had them pick up the little boys. Turns out, the older one. When they broke the news of the fatality, they knew of no such child. This kid, he's a John Doe. We don't even know what he was doing here tonight. I'm pretty sure they suspect the old lady; but, currently she's hysterical. Off on-" he said.

"Do you suspect her?" I said.

"I don't know. I don't know nothing, none of-" he said.

"HEY What're you doing! Freelancing?! Greenburg! Stephanopolopodopolous! Get back over here!"

"Stephanopolopodopolous?" I said.

"What? It's Greek," he said.

"Is that normal for him?" I asked.

"Nah, guess horrible things like this just do that to him," he said.

"Oh good! I was about to say that he's getting more and more like my last boss every day," I said.

"*Gay or straight; boys will be boys*"

Chapter Seven

It was a very dark night. Not really storming though. It was sprinkling. Not enough to really soak everything, just enough to get everything wet. The worst possible driving conditions. You see, the roads have oil in them. And whenever it rains, the water draws out the oil and makes it slick. But this was a mild rain. Unlike a major thunderstorm, it wasn't enough to rinse away the oil, just enough to draw it out. And to make matters worse. It was about as dark as it could be in the city. It was the middle of a new moon, and very overcast. Wasn't a dot of light in the sky. Don't even think I saw a plane; though I wasn't looking.

We knew it was bad, like, really bad. Even for firefighters, we rushed there as fast as we could. It was very late, Friday night. Suddenly out of seemingly nowhere a Hasidic Jew seemed to appear. Or maybe it took that long for us to be able to see him. Regardless, he was dressed in the traditional dress. Which is very dark. And no doubt walking home from synagogue, it was after dark so the next day had begun. Which is why there was synagogue in the first place. But unfortunately this is also the same night that the drunk gentiles are out. Ugh. We swerved and narrowly avoided hitting him; but we did take out a street sign. How he didn't see us; I'll never know. A fire engine, with lights and sirens blaring. That's the opposite of hard to see. We were glad that we didn't hit him; imagine if we had. And at a time like this! We didn't have time to assess the damage. Though I'll tell you right now, we later had to explain it to Mr. Patfield and the vehicle technicians; because you could clearly see the damage to the fire truck. We weren't making any turns, just going straight down the road, so we were going faster than we probably should have been. After that we did however go a bit slower. Not like all the way down to speed limit, believe me. But, as I have explained, the roads were very slick.

It was a bad time to begin with. We were the first to arrive because we were what was available. I had been having a bad day already to begin with. But, personal matters not worth relating, least of all here. It was only a few blocks left. Soon, we arrived. The house was found exclusively based on the house numbers painted on the curb. There was no sign of it being on fire, our first break. And probably the last one of the night.

We burst in. The house seemed empty, not abandoned, but empty. We doubted that anyone would answer the door. But we didn't break down the door. It was not only unlocked, but when I went to open it (feeling if it was hot) it wasn't even fully shut. Just pulled to enough that it looked closed. It may be an unusually safe city, but not that safe. That was suspicious and concerning.

Immediately upon opening the door I could smell burnt flesh. "*Oh no.*" Suddenly I was remembering the Madison storm. It was horrible. But, it wasn't quite the same smell. Accelerant? I didn't smell blood. I had to press ahead. I was one that stood outside in case things went wrong. Before that we all had to layout initial water connection. As you may know from your homeowner's insurance. If you have a fire hydrant in front of your house, then you will have a discount on your homeowner's insurance. This was not such a house. It was smack in the middle of a block. Could it get any worse? But soon was the hand jack and they were in the house with the hoses.

It was only a minute later that they had us come in. The initial attack was all that was needed to put out the fire. It was an old house. Old hardwood floors, original fixtures. It was the opposite of the first house fire I was up against. But, that's about where the good news ends. I went right into the room where the fire had been. It was freaky. Besides having had a fire, well, I could tell it hadn't been engulfed, that much we got there in time. But. It was scary. It felt like there had been a fire at Enigma Haunted house. There were chains, and restraints, and more disturbing devices I am not about to describe. I could tell that it was a bedroom. I also noticed bottles of motor oil. Within context they fit in. Then I noticed IT. At first glance I had not paid too much attention to the thing in the middle of the floor. Then I realized, it was not an it. It was a who. It was horrible to see. The burns on his body seemed 100%. I was barely able to do my job. But, we pressed ahead. The pain he must have been in. It must have been unbearable. It got worse. I realized it was not a man. It was a kid. I could tell also that it was a boy. We radioed all this in. So that the Next Due Squad would have advanced notice. There were already more coming. But, this way there would be a better picture. And an understanding that this was mainly a call for paramedics. We had no stretcher, and as you know. Technically there is no such thing as a 4th degree burn. But, if there was, this might be it. It took three horrible minutes for EMR to arrive. I can still clearly see him in my mind. His charred skin. Burnt flesh visible and portions of his body that normally would be well concealed under skin. We worked hard and fast to cool him down. With any burn, the flesh is still the burn temperature. So you have to cool it down to stop the cooking. But, for all people might expect him to be black and charred like ash. Not so much. In fact, his charred flesh was actually very pale. It was a horrible sight. He was naked so there was no clothing sticking to his flesh; to be removed and take the skin off with

Finally, paramedic backup arrived. They were more prepared for a medical emergency then we were. But, we remained partially as all-hands-on-deck, we were also trained in that. Also, we were there on Re-flash watch just in case the fire started again. To this day I am glad I was on guard instead of being sent in. I can only imagine what that scene must have been

"Whoa," said one.

"Mild compared to that one few weeks back on Coconut Palm Road," said another.

"Don't Yap! Work!" said the supervisor.

"Outside, looks like a case of shock. You'd better go check it out," said another.

As you can imagine, it was pretty bad, bad enough that we must have missed it. I stepped outside. And I found him on the front porch. He was about 13, maybe 14. He was also naked. What was going on?! I could clearly tell he was in shock. Shock wanders, maybe he wandered off when we arrived and then came back. It may have been late, but it was over 80°. I put my coat over him. It was cliché shock. Or, perhaps "textbook" would be the more accurate word. I didn't go back to the truck to get a blanket for fear that he'd wander. I radioed it in for a second ambulance.

I started talking to him, to keep him with me.

"Hi, what's your name?" I said.

"Dave," he said.

"*Good, he's with it enough to communicate*. How are you feeling?"

He yawned and said, "Thirsty, maybe a little queasy."

"So, what happened?" I asked.

"I, it, it was an accident," he said.

"An accident?" I said.

"I, it, it all just happened so fast, I-I-I-I-"

"That's ok," he said, "Just, well, it's going to be ok,"

"He's gunu be ok?!" he said, perking up slightly.

I paused. Technically I didn't know for sure that he wasn't going to survive. Even if he did, would horrific burns but surviving still count as ok? I didn't know. We don't really have Life Flight here in Boca Raton. Yet still, he might be flown out to Miami. Not knowing what else to do. And technically not being totally false, I said "I do not have that information."

"You mean you don't know?" I said.

"We got a whole big team of people working on him. I'm just here to take care of you," I said.

"So, who is he?" I asked.

"He?" Dave asked.

"You know, the obvious," I said.

"He, he," he said hesitant, "he's my boyfriend."

Suddenly it hit me like a ton of bricks. Of course! It all made sense. It was a freaky room, full of freaky things. But, it seemed a little off. Something about it. That's what it was! Let us just say I didn't catch it at first because I'm not into that sort of thing. It all made sense! Certainly explained the candles. Which is no doubt how it started. Dave wasn't covered in motor oil, but he was. Just got too close to one of the candles, and well. I can confirm Dave wasn't burned.

"I-I, I mean, what's his name?" I said.

"Gabe," he said.

"Stay with me, stay awake," I said.

He sighed.

"Stay with me, talk to me. I can't let you go to sleep," I said, I tapped him on the shoulder, trying to jolt him.

"Talk about what?" he said.

"Well, just what all happened?" I said.

"How did it happen?" he asked.

"Yes,"

"Where should I begin?" he said.

"Oh, how about at the very beginning," I said.

"Oh, how it began initially…" It is at that point that I wish to simply relay, shall I say, a reader's digest version of what happened. He told me how they first met. It was in school, people were figuring out that he was gay. At home that was ok. But at school. And he didn't say how they were figuring it out. But, at school, well. He was getting bullied bad, real bad. And since the faculty's jobs were not contingent on keeping it under control. Well, he went light on that whole part of the story. But, someday he had just snapped. Gabe been really bad, particularly mean and a bullying leader. And he just lunged at him, using the element of surprise and stuck his tongue down Gabe's throat. At the time he had thought that that was that. And after that things would be, well. He never said (one way or the other) if it was so at school. But, it was after that that it got really obscene. Even for a teenage boy of any orientation! I wouldn't have believed him, but for what I had seen. We talked for a good while, I was keeping him talking and it was something for him to stay conscious talking about. I stayed with him not just till an ambulance for him arrived, but I even ended up going with him to Boca Raton Regional hospital. In order to keep this book from becoming E.L. James Comes Out of the Closet, I won't be relaying any of it here. Suffice to say what little there was that wasn't utterly, well, it was a little like a stereotypical dopey romantic comedy, except for the obvious of course. In time they got caught, ironically in Dave's closet. They didn't quite know what they had walked in on. They thought it was rape. And so, no one had known anything about Gabe, so Dave played along. He had been through enough and didn't want to have Gabe go through that. Naturally Dave had been arrested. I was guessing the time in jail, he didn't do so well. He had just been bailed out. I was guessing earlier that day at that. Well, he had decided to try and put together something nice for them. Undisputedly they had been through a lot. He said that it wasn't quite as nice as the place they had had on Coconut Palm Road where they had gotten caught. But, well, he had found this place available, and the rest is history.

By this time we had been talking for some time, and I was now at the hospital. That was the end of my shift.

"Stephanopolopodopolous! Boy am I glad to run into you," I said.

"And I you," he said, "How was it?"

"Meh, been better been worse," I said.

"I'm worried the shock is the least of the worries," he said.

"I'm pretty sure it is," I said.

"Yeah, probably," he said.

"How you holding up?" I said.

"Oh, it's, it's, is, it's, it reminds me. Of, of this case. The overall haunting of it. Dealing with people, though with the best ultimate intensions. They do horrible things. And they don't understand what they've done. They simply can't wrap their head around it. It's kinda-sorta not even their fault. I mean, it's almost a disability. They don't, they won't they probably never will! And, and, it's just so horrible to see-"

"That teen suicide-" I said.

"Yeah, in fact now that you mention it. That's a shining example. But no. No it was one of the few police horrors I dealt with in San Francisco.

"What happened?" I said.

"Was a rich kid, ended up in trouble. I remember it clearly, err, more clearly than I'd like. She was powerless. Exposed. There was nothing she could do. They even had said as they put her in holding 'Sorry, the Ritz Carlton was full.' It was horrible her treatment. The powerlessness. I knew of it. She pulled against the handcuffs, wanting, powerlessly to merely scratch their face. Not really much comparatively, probably wouldn't even pull that off. But they were metal and strong. Sure it was vengeful. But, there was nothing she could do. There was no discipline of the officers. Let alone any prosecution. There never was any anything! They hurt her, and life just went on. I, it's a horrifying memory. But, I guess that's why police officers undermine rights and do what it takes to get convictions. Seeing things, horrible things. And, nothing happens, they won't feel guilt. They won't feel bad. They can't understand what they have done. They just abuse their power and then clock out to think about dinner. Maybe even get praised-"

"What was the crime allegation?" I said.

"Eh, who cares! Didn't ask, didn't care," he said.

"I'm, I'm sorry. I shouldn't have asked that-" I said.

"Meh, don't care! So what if you shouldn't have. I just, so much. So many things. Things that matter and are significant. Not molehills made into mountains, I just stop caring," he said.

"Just, umm, how should I ask- well, umm, did, did she hang herself in jail?" I said.

"No, it was minor, at least the physical injuries I could treat. No, what happened was she pulled so hard against the handcuffs. Every fiber, every part of her body crying out for, revenge, for justice, for SOMETHING. Ultimately fueled by the fiery powerlessness of knowing it was impossible, that it couldn't and wouldn't ever happen. Guess that was her first time being arrested. The real issue, it was within, the experience-" he said.

"The psychological effect of it all," I said.

"Yeah," he said, guess that's probably a little more scientific," I said.

"Yeah, well, meh, how you holding up?" he said.

"As well as could be expected. It was horrible the sight. I can't imagine the agonizing pain-" I said.

"Greenburg you know as well as I do with how the nerves get charred, he may not have been in any pain at all! At, at least not yet," he said.

"Oh yeah, whoa, that's a relief," I said, "Course, got a long road ahead."

"Well," he said.

"Did He Not Survive!" I said.

"All I can say for certainty is that he was alive when my leg of medical treatment was ended," he said.

"Oh," I said.

"And your end?" he said.

"I, as I said, the medical end over here is the least of my worries," I said.

"Indeed, just, is this just what I am to deal with? Will my career simply consist of such horrors? I saw Space City. We had a case like that down there. Before my time, But I had found a news story about it in my youth. Guy, was like 22, but when he was 13 he had at least allegedly raped another boy. Then like 2 weeks later set him on fire trying to kill him. Cover up. At least they didn't put him in jail, make him go through all that while he was still a teenager. But, at the time I thought, it gave me cause for pause. Guess I never forgot It." he paused and said "It haunts me. I will never forget in the news report how they said they were moving onto the sentencing phase and the words 'how many decades he will get.' Err, something like that. Human mind remembers the gist of things, not good about word-for-word. They had said that his lawyer had said that you probably will be convicted just because of emotions. But, they crazy part is, as I recall. It was like this poor little boy, all the treatments and all he went through. They were the same age as I recall. Seemed to me mostly like, and I may not know what I am talking about but, it seemed to me like just some teenage boy, albeit taken to the absolute extreme. And then followed by some scared kid," he said.

"Heard a similar case out of Houston, young boy got caught with his first girlfriend. Was no murder or murder attempts, but, they got him in adult court-" I said.

"Don't remember that one," he said.

"It was the first domino to a lot of stuff, that one case," I said.

"Yeah, well. I saw THAT, and I have seen things. Crazy, horrible things, maybe, it's all just catching up to me," he said.

"You came to Florida. To get away, from crazy things?" I said.

"Well, well, so did you! At least I'm a paramedic. I came expecting nothing but heart attacks, falls, you know. Old people calls," he said.

"Yes, but for all the stereotype, people over the age of 65 make up only a fifth of this city," I said.

"But the hospital is the largest employer in the city. And, it, it's, It's just, I have gotten out of-" he said.

"Oh please! Houston's just a place with a high concentration of refineries, and astronauts! Sure there's been some crazy corruption come to light. But, what they did. All put together. The single largest thing to separate what happened out in Texas was that they had to put someone into their police's internal affairs that was really willing to stand up, to fight the horrific, the even, even the lawful corruption," I said.

That struck a nerve.

"I'm sorry, I didn't mean for you to-" I said.

"De nada," he said, "I'm sure you're right. Guess, well, if you don't see the proof, well, you can show yourself plausible deniability. So much easier to sit down at a café, and dip biscotti in your drink if you're not thinking about how some minor kid is locked away somewhere, right that minute,"

By this time we had walked down and were about out. As most anyone knows, there's always a cop in a hospital. I overheard the officer talking to another about the case.

"I'll catch up to you," I said.

"Umm, officer," I said.

"What!" he said, clearly irritated at being interrupted and acting it.

"I have a statement about the Dave-Gabe case. I don't know the last names," I said.

"Oh," he said, possibly as a question.

"The one we brought in with the shock," I said. I was quite obviously a firefighter.

"Oh?" he said, his interest peaked.

"He's innocent," I said.

"What!" he said.

"They were an under-the-table gay couple-" I said.

"I am in the middle of a conversation!" he said.

Stephanopolopodopolous jumped in, "Oh come on! I saw rose petals on the bed!-" he said cut off.

"Firemen please! I am in the middle of work. This conversation is over. Now don't you have somewhere to be?" he said forcefully.

I tried to speak, but I was cut off "But-" And so, like that. That was that. Now I was the powerless one. He couldn't understand, he wouldn't understand. He wouldn't even listen. But, I did have one concession. I was being shoved out of a place, instead of in one.

"Proof?" said Stephanopolopodopolous.

"Proof."

"*1. The visible heat and light emanating from any body during the process of its combustion or burning. 2. Any combustible body in a state of ignition or heated to a redness. 3. Fuel in a state of combustion, as in a stove, grate, or furnace, on a hearth, or on or in the ground; a mass a material lighted and burning for the sake of the warmth it affords, or for the use of its heat in cooking, etc. 4. The burning of a house or other building or of a town, forest, etc.: as, a fire in a crowded block; the great fire of Chicago; a prairie fire.*" –Webster's New Twentieth Dictionary of the English Language Unabridged Standard Reference Works Publishing Company, Ink. New York 1957

Chapter Eight

After that event I had to take some time off. I left the emergency room, by all rights in a huff. Man I was mad. I don't like getting that angry. I have learned from Stephanopolopodopolous how human memory deteriorates. And fast. Would be a sleepless night anyway so I checked into Quality Inn. But before that I stopped off at CVS and picked up some tablets. The paper kind. And pens. I thought that if only they knew, if I could tell that story, well. I quickly got to work. It disgusted me. But, it was what I could do for him. After that I did something of a second draft, fixing grammatical and Syntactic mistakes mostly. But also making notes of portions wherein I believed myself to have first been wrong. But, that doesn't mean much later on revisions. First time out of the gate is far more accurate. But, nevertheless I also worried. About how in the retrieval of memory, that alone can change it. The brain is actually pulling data from different parts of the brain. Trying to recreate it from that. And to further complicate things, if you don't revisit memory. There goes the pathway to the memory. Ergo, you forget. So I was in a Catch 22. But I worked quick. And hard. In the revision of what I had written, then it hit me the extreme obscenity of what I had written. I had to get copies made. For safety in case something happened to the manuscript. I couldn't have a printer come out to the hotel room. So I had to run the risk of taking it out. Fortunately it wasn't raining, but it was still a bit moist out. I had to be cautious. I was really worried. Knowing what I was holding. At Minuteman Press I had to be very discrete, I didn't need people knowing just what I was printing. Even having it made me a little nervous. It was true and intended for the purpose of criminal defense. But it was young boys. Enough so that I doubted that publication would even is legal. Certainly the last thing I would be going for. I made 10 copies (of both the original and the revision). It scared me so much when a page tore out horribly wrong at Minuteman press. But I kept it under wraps and put the tablet into the copier with the torn off part. Was able to print it readably. Sure there were some junk pages, those I wasn't about to chunk there.

(insert mule picture here)
Houston•Barrow•San Francisco•Upstate New York•Boca Raton

I got three different safety deposit boxes at 3 completely different banks. In each I held 2 copies. The original and the original revision both went into SDBs but not together in the same. 2 I kept in my residence. And the rest (2) I kept at the firehouse. The firehouse copies promptly disappeared. I was too scared to ask questions. And, as you know. I, right now, lie here dictating this whole book to a staff member, for reasons I will explain later on. My house has already been cleared out, and for personal reasons I'm pretty sure there went those copies. One bank location. It was ruined in the appropriately named hurricane you probably already know of, hurricane with old woman's name. Bank took on water. Made the mistake of taking a low level SDB on the first floor for the purpose of storing papers. Another bank branch I have lost that SBD. There went that. All that remains is 1. Like all the others it holds 2 copies. Neither are the original hand written or the original hand written revision. Instead it holds 2 copies of both. Readable (but probably not easily). All this time. Throughout the rest of this book from here on out, past the end of this book, the whole time I've been in this burn ward, the whole entire time I've been working on this. Dave has been locked in jail. Adult jail at that no doubt. I swore I'd stand for him. I'd testify. I'd follow news reports, though what they did to my heart rhythm. (And I'm not even someone with heart problems) But, here I lie. His trial is coming up. Yeah, speedy trial my eye. I said I'd testify, I'd recount that night, and well. I won't make it. I'll tell you that right up now. As a non-secquotor, I knew I wouldn't last too long. And as such I made the mistake you have already no doubt come across in the first chapter. I jumped ahead just-in-case I didn't live long enough to, well. As they say, meanwhile back at the ranch. But the written word in question, that I had already done before you-will-see happened. And there it lies. Much like me, but I have an expiration date. Will it be enough? Will it be ruled inadmissible? Thereby silenced? Will They Even Know of it at All?! I've made phone calls (with assistance.) I've done what I can, which is next to squat.

(insert mule picture here)
Houston•Barrow•San Francisco•Upstate New York•Boca Raton

(insert fire and flames here)

When the call came in, me and Stephanopolopodopolous were talking about a personal matter.

"You went through the sailor-suit-thing-photo-shoot as a kid too?" he said.

"Oh yes," I said.

"I thought that it wasn't any more mortifying than having to wear a dress. Few years later I'd get confirmation," he said.

"They thought you looked like a cute little boy in a dress?!" I said shocked and having trouble believing. That seemed more like something a vengeful adult child would to do a horrible father / elder now being cared for.

"No, middle school gym. Had my clothes stolen. Not that they did anything about it," he said.

And before we got to school uniforms, the call came in:

(insert fire and flames here)

Gladys had put the tea kettle on. When she stopped in Dollar Tree, she normally wasn't one for green tea. But she couldn't resist the bargain. 100 tea bags for $1. After sales tax that's only $1.07. When she got home the first thing she did was put on the kettle. Then she put her purchases away. After that she had to rest on the couch. She quickly fell asleep. Now, for just one little cup of tea, she didn't insert much water into the kettle. And it might have been a whistling tea kettle, but she was hard of hearing. It's also worth noting that she had forgotten to put the whistler down.

As is the normal case in almost all apartments, the stove was an electric with a swirling burner. And it was up very high. As you would expect, it didn't take long for all the H_2O to evaporate away. Now, when an electric burner is left on, with nothing on it. Eventually with nothing for it to act on, it will melt down. That is certainly the case with Immersion water heaters plugged in unsubmersed. Now, when a stove is left going with nothing but an empty kettle to act on. For it to melt down with. Well that's a fire.

(insert fire and flames here)

It didn't seem like that unusual a call. I do admit that I've had worse. Apartment fire. Explosion reported. Firefighters already on scene. But they had called for us as backup. We rushed over, an apartment fire. Relatively day to day.

(insert fire and flames here)

Unbeknown to Gladys. She lived right next door to a drug lab. On the same side of her apartment as her electric stove. And as you probably would imagine, it wasn't Bristol-Myers Squibb. It was the kind you go to jail for. And, among other things, they are notorious for blowing up. Like many, this one dealt with flammable things. Things producing very flammable gases.

It only took but the littlest of flame to ignite the gases. The ignition was instantaneously an explosion. An explosion stereotypical of an action movie. The

(insert mule picture here)

windows burst out in clouds of flame. The door opened inward, so that it didn't fly open. It was only a fraction of a second for it to be completely engulfed in fire. An inferno really. Killing the drug dealers working inside.

The fire got through the adjacent wall back into Gladys' apartment very fast. There was a smoke detector, but didn't wake Gladys. Probably couldn't have anyway. It was the explosion itself. Whether it was the sound, or feeling the force (or possibly both). Shall never be known. Regardless, Gladys was jolted awake. As quick as she could (which wasn't very fast) she grabbed the keys. And headed out the door.

On the far side of the lab a family lived. It was an end apartment, and that was fortunate because the far side was where the daughters had decided (fits and tantrums involved) that they would have their beds. It was also fortunate (though embarrassing) that that was when the mom had decided to grab a quick shower. The dad was also in the bathroom with her, where he had been spending much time, in order to prepare for a colonoscopy.

There was a hose out front. Carelessly (though fortunately) the last person to be in need of this hose had not actually bothered to turn the water off. Instead a sprayer attachment was attached and they simply disengaged the trigger, hadn't even bothered to properly coil it.

A neighbor in the building directly across had been lying awake with insomnia. He heard the explosion. At first he didn't realize it wasn't his own building. Grabbed a towel to hide his nakedness as quick as he could and darted out the door. He then noticed Gladys, he didn't know her. Didn't even remember having seen her. But he noticed she was on fire, then the hose. He quickly grabbed a garden hose and sprayed her with it.

At first Gladys was scared. But she couldn't really much get away from him anyway. And she quickly realized what he was doing.

In the apartment behind the lab, a bachelor for life was moving out. He had already packed up all his belongings. Unfortunately for him, the movers were set to come in the morning, not this evening. He himself was sitting up watching WPBF. He got out safely.

A coven of witches ran out of the apartment directly above the lab. One moment they were in the midst of religious rituals, the next they were immersed. They could fell it though the floor. By the time the last wiccan's foot was on soil, all the lab's adjacent apartments were swallowed up.

(insert fire and flames here)

We were almost there. I could see the smoke coming up off the complex. At first they had said All companies Working. But soon they realized that wasn't enough, and called for backup.

(insert fire and flames here)

Of the four apartments immediately adjacent to the lab, there were 5 apartments which were in turn immediately adjacent to two of the four. One that was above Gladys' apartment and next door to the one above the lab. And likewise-inverse on the other side. There was one apartment behind Gladys' and next door to the apartment behind

(insert mule picture here)
Houston•Barrow•San Francisco•Upstate New York•Boca Raton

the lab. Once again, likewise on the far side. And a 5th above the apartment behind the lab and behind the apartment above the lab. Of those five, all were soon on fire.

But what of the apartment behind the apartment above Gladys' apartment? And likewise on the mirror side? The two apartments which shared a 3 dimensional geometric corner with the lab. What of those? Well in one an old man simply pressed the button on his Personal Emergency Response System from Boca Home Care Services. The force of the explosion had knocked him down getting up off the toilet. As for the other apartment, well…

Alexander Kafka (no relation to the writer or the great) was an odd man who kept odd hours and had even stranger habits. He wasn't really that old person in the neighborhood that never ever leaves and always keeps the drapes shut, behind which he was doing things unknown. But he was as close as you can ever come in an apartment complex, which is pretty close. Also he wasn't really a crotchety old man, he just lived like one; he was only 29 after all. He had been preparing (or perhaps embellishing would be a more accurate word) his lunch at the time of the explosion. Like many people listed here, he lived alone. When the blast first happened. He poo-poo-ed it. Soon afterward flames started to appear in a corner of his back bed room. His smoke detector when ott. He at first thought it was a mistake, simply assuming it to be so, just like that employee in the MGM Grand Hotel Fire. But, soon he realized otherwise. He grabbed an extinguisher, extinguished it a little, then pulled out the nightstand, and finished it off. He exhausted the main extinguisher and had to dip into the second. He was so glad he had gotten second extinguisher. He knew it was dangerous, but he didn't want to lose his beloved (although derelict) residence. He heard people shouting, banging on his door, even once throwing something through his window. That too he poo-poo-ed. But when he heard the fire wagon's siren. Then the real possibility of the danger hit him. He stepped out onto the balcony. Then he knew just how bad it was. He could no longer stand his ground and protect his residence. Twice already he had had to re-spray a different spot in that corner. He ruched and grabbed a few prized possessions, then ran out and down the stairs.

(insert fire and flames here)

When we arrived a significant effort was already underway. Seeing those that had had to flee their homes, it was clear that they had been caught completely off guard. So far only two injuries, but one person that we had had to save. However, the nucleus was too hot. And it was quite clear, just from looking, what was the nucleus.

Hoses were already hooked up, the building was being cleared. Efforts were underway already to make sure it didn't spread to the other buildings. It wasn't a good apartment complex. It wasn't a large apartment complex. The entire complex was square in shape. And had a total of 4 buildings, set out like rows. They were identical except that one apartment in the building facing the street was built to instead be the office. In front of the street was a parking lot, and was the visitor parking. The first two buildings had a common yard, not well maintained. There was a parking lot between the second and the third building. And a second run-amuck, nasty yard between the third building, and the building on fire. And behind the burning building, there was another small lot. The entire complex was built on the end of a block, the only way I can even say front was that it was small residential streets on both sides. There was no fence anywhere. Probably one of the worst housing complexes in Boca Raton. But, there were some big trees. Behind the complex was residential housing. Houses. Which also had some big trees. It was enough that the trees overhung each other, their branches often intertwined.

Hoses were already hooked up. There wasn't much left of the main burning building to clear. Sure we were checking the entire complex, but there wasn't that many that hadn't heard the sound. A few times there was an issue, not anyone we had to force out of their apartment. Naturally there was no one in the office. Of course, who would be working in a leasing office at that time of night?

We were told that the place was not well maintained, certainly not prepared for a fire. Only 1 in five apartments it even seemed had a smoke detector. Pathetic. Also this was a fast and rapidly expanding fire. Smoke was coming out of neighboring backyards. We were sent in.

Now, Boca Raton may be an unusually safe place, but nevertheless people here in Boca Raton get nervous and scared (like anyone else) when they hear people rustling around in their backyard at night, and that's all they know. I was one of the firefighters to go up to the door.

G-R-A-N-K-!-! I turned the doorbell handle to ring.

"FIRE DEPARTMENT!" one of us shouted out.

It took a moment for there to be an answer. But only a moment. An older-late-middle-aged woman answered the door. She was wearing a bathrobe, and looked like she had just been woken out of a sound sleep. One thing was clear, she was caught off guard and had not known of the fire.

"We regret to inform you ma'am that your backyard is on fire," said the superior, speaking fast soasto get back there faster.

"What?" she said half asleep.

"That explosion you heard, err, slept through, it set those apartments on fire. The fire's spreading fast, we believe it's in your backyard," he said.

"Fire? There's a fire?" she said.

"Please evacuate the house," said the superior. "You may want to quickly gather some essential and vital possessions."

"What?!" she said, beginning to wake up.

The driveway of the house ran right alongside the fence, the fence was the property line with the apartments. It did lead to a garage. We had known about the garage thanks to Google's services for fire departments. But, it didn't lead straight to the garage, once you passed the house, the driveway curved. The garage was more centered between the two sides of the property. Going up the driveway was a Cadillac parked in the driveway, close to the garage in the yard was parked a big van. Behind the house was a more lemon Cadillac and an even more run down pick-up. Behind the house the yard was a mess. It had more trees than most backyards would. And it wasn't really mowed or raked to speak of. Underbrush, if you will. And to make matters worse. It was just straight up filthy. There was litter that probably made its way from the apartment complex and junk items lying around. And some items such as gas cans that we couldn't tell if they even were intended to be there, or they just left trashy junk lying around. The whole atmosphere of it all, in a word. It just felt very dense. All together it was a terrible place to be fighting a fire. The good news was that while it was raging in the complex. Here it had just begun.

Smash!

Think again. A diseased branch fell through the roof of the garage. It was one of the largest branches, guess not much burning was enough to take it down. Then we heard a scream. Was someone working late at something in the garage? We looked inside. It had been converted into a garage apartment, and it looked like the home base for some rock band. In fact the branch had landed on a set of drums. The man door to the garage had a window. Very dirty, but you could kinda see through it. I saw the person in there. It was a young guy, about 30. He was wearing a black tee shirt. But, embarrassingly, nothing else. It was quite clear. Trying to make it in something you never will. Not being able to survive on your own, no one wanting to hire you. Being helplessly and completely dependent. Still living with (or perhaps under would be more accurate) your parents. Having to have their permission for everything. Them always knowing what you're doing, always having a superior. Someone watching over you. Twoo Twoo. My worst nightmare. Well, after prison, and military rule, and dystopia and etc…

We broke the door down, or forced it open might be more accurate. (It was very flimsy.) We got him out just in time. Passing through I could see that, while they had not room for cars in the garage. They had not only let the clutter and filth of the back yard drift into the garage apartment. But they had also more garage items, and items that were very flammable. By the time we had all gotten out, it had begun to really get going in the garage.

We stepped back out into the overgrown and filthy backyard. Then a spot was noticed. It was what had been a pretty green clump, but there must have been some sort of a chemical spill. It now looked like someone had started a strong and healthy campfire. This backyard was about to go up, and it was going to take the house with it.

We went back up front. And yes, we did get him a towel.

"Is the house cleared?" was asked. Now there were 3 people out front.

"Yes, but, can we go back ins-"

"NO! There's a rapidly expanding fire in the back. It's going to take the house,"

"What?!"

"We're doing what we can, but it's a big apartment fire over there, and it's spread over to here."

"*When you choose the lesser of two evils, always remember that it is still an evil*" - Max Lerner

Chapter Nine

It was my very next shift at the firehouse. I still hadn't been on too long. Still was figuring out some of the ropes. Now I had been there a while. It wasn't like I didn't know where the bathrooms were. (Down the hall, first door, right men's, women's left.) In police terms I was in my rookie year.

"I thought that the number one rule was that the firehouse not burn down," I said.

"Pah, firehouse burn down, well that's kind of an extreme-"

"Don't knock it, it happened in Ionia New York, and to the Wildcat fire station in Georgia amid a violent storm-"

"Happened to the Ohio county fire department in Kentucky."

"Even across the street from Knott's berry farm there's a burnt out firehouse."

"Happened in Walnutport-"

(insert fire and flames here)

Boca Raton is said to be the Beverly Hills of Florida. It's also said that it's hard to find a community that isn't gated. Personally I hate those, it's not like that they have so much more than we do, it's just. Places, places and things that think they simply have the authority to keep out those they don't want, well. Meanwhile back at the Beverly Hills of Florida, certain things accompany wealth. Caviar, expensive cars, big houses, professional-certified-public-accountants-filing-your-taxes, boats, but also expensive restaurants. Once again, places that think they simply have the authority to keep out those they don't want. People that have to ask prices, children. But, not in this case. Or maybe he had some connection. Regardless. But, just as every good thing has some downside. Every bad thing has some upside. Such was the case with the rule about children.

(insert fire and flames here)

The alarm went off. And that was the end of that conversation.

(insert fire and flames here)

(insert mule picture here)
Houston•Barrow•San Francisco•Upstate New York•Boca Raton

Though rarely obeyed, technically children (particularly small children) and tablecloths should not be. Deal is, children can pull on them, they can pull things down. Down onto themselves. I know that pets on medication that makes them food crazed certainly can do that. But, children, tablecloths, and combustion. Well now. That's a whole other class of danger.

(insert fire and flames here)

Outside the firehouse yellow lights blink on streetlights at almost all times, you've probably seen this before. Likely not at this specific firehouse. But at firehouses where you life. Night, day, holiday. With one exception. When there's an emergency it's replaced with a dual red light. We switched it to red, and we were off.

(insert fire and flames here)

The order arrived. It wasn't the most expensive thing on the menu. But they knew that that's what they had wanted. The flambé was lit.

(insert fire and flames here)

I knew what was in store. At this point any last hope of Dave getting bail was out the window; the judge had flatly denied it. Frankly, we had known that all along. But, well, like Stephanopolopodopolous said "If you don't see the proof you can show yourself plausible deniability." Everything about that call was horrible. What he must be going through. To be in jail at that age! To be going through that trauma from behind bars!! In the words of Morton salt "when it rains, it pours." And the idea, of that boy. Having to spend decades, or the rest of his life. Even if he was guilty. It's just so unfair to have to serve that kind of time for something you did at that age. Well, guess one reason why there had better be an afterlife. And there had better be a hell for the law enforcement that do such horrible things. He had only one hope, we all know what it was. And even at that, even if acquitted. Probably come out not just screwed up, but a delinquent simply because of the whole experience. He wouldn't stay out from behind bars no matter what.

But now, I was headed into that again, after it was the first time I had had to take time off since arriving at BRFD. Now this one was without the obvious of course. But still. It was a horrific call even without PAAA.

(insert fire and flames here)

They said it was so good. It smelled good. He couldn't wait. Parents were excited. They weren't the only ones. They said it was a big celebration. Well, maybe he could pull it closer, pull himself up to see.

(insert fire and flames here)

We were almost there. Ready or not. Here I come.

(insert fire and flames here)

(insert mule picture here)
Houston•Barrow•San Francisco•Upstate New York•Boca Raton

The boy cried out in pain. Throughout the restaurant people jumped up literally. The mother rushed it beat it out. Two different people tossed their drinks at him. A third man poured hard liquor on him. He screamed louder. The father punched him out. He had to protect his boy! The tablecloth caught on. A waiter was running panicked not able to think. He spread it to another table. People were scrambling to and fro. A real-visible scramble-spiral. Like a dictator or in a police interrogation. People were confused, not sure what to do, how to protect themselves, how to save others, even pitted against each other. It was a truly horrible sight.

(insert fire and flames here)

We pulled the apparatus into the parking lot.

(insert fire and flames here)

Finally a chef had been able to come to his senses. He rushed out into the dining area with a large red fire extinguisher.

(insert fire and flames here)

The structure fire was out by the time we arrived. It had been caught in time before it of itself had been that bad. And it wasn't my first such burn obviously. Nevertheless, well. I pressed ahead. There were multiple injuries. But all but the obvious were minor burns. One person, in it all had spilled on themself the melted wax of a candle that had been burning for a long time. We went straight to the primary victim. He was much younger than Gabe. Much less burned. A lot of epidermis had been destroyed. But much more dermis was no doubt intact. And not all of him was burned at all. It wasn't like it was a minor case at all. Don't get me wrong; let's get that straight up front. But, well, I guess that (name) isn't quite so bad as (name). He would survive, it wouldn't be nearly as disfigured. His recovery would be less.

"*From even the greatest of horrors, Irony is seldom absent*" - H. P. Lovecraft

Chapter Ten

The young boy from pervious was taken to the hospital. I went back to my fire barn. (what? My first position I was as much as anything simply support for rural departments.) And so, life, at least for me, began to go back to normal. A more day-to-day burn case. A more day-to-day car accident. A more day-to-day house fire. For me, things were finally stabilizing.

(insert fire and flames here)

.

(insert mule picture here)

Houston•Barrow•San Francisco•Upstate New York•Boca Raton

An older man falls to the floor. He clutches his chest and wheezes.

(insert fire and flames here)

"Indeed, you know he's on the fire department color guard?"

"Not surprised. Seems more and more like my first supervisor by the day. Course, not as bad. Not to that degree, Certainly I'd pick this supervisor over that one any day," I said.

"Yeah, and also he's been here a while. If he was going to go to what I think you fear, I think that he would have done it by now."

"Well, he's pretty older. How long has he been here?" I asked.

"Practically since the forest fire by Floresta," he said kiddingly.

"Shiesh."

(insert fire and flames here)

Funeral plans were made for the older man. Like many families, they had him cremated for money's sake.

(insert fire and flames here)

"I can't believe this," said Stephanopolopodopolous.

"I'm still in shock over the Dave-Gabe thing. But, I've come to the conclusion that just as Floridians will be Floridians, those in power will be those in power. For Pete's sake, back, way back in the 20's when our very first fire engine was still in use as a day-to-day fire engine for Emergency Service use. The fire chief, being top banana. He had the fire engine repainted to match his white hair," I said.

"You have got to be kidding me," said Stephanopolopodopolous.

"That's what I said when I was told. Those very words, in that very order, probably even in that very same tone of voice," I said.

"But, well, well that I guess just goes to show Florida has always been Florida and no doubt will always be Florida. But, this? Can you believe this?" said Stephanopolopodopolous.

"Dude, I was there at the Madison Storm. I have no problem believing that someone would be thrown into an asthma attack from the experience of dealing with a cop," I said.

"But, I mean come on. Asthma is the airways seizing up! Often caused by allergies-" said Stephanopolopodopolous

"But not this time, this time it was emotions. But, her reaching for something. Probably thought it was merciful just tazering her. Which when someone is in urgent need of their inhalator, that's probably the absolute worst thing you can do." I said.

(insert fire and flames here)

The undertaker prepares the body for cremation.

(insert mule picture here)
Houston•Barrow•San Francisco•Upstate New York•Boca Raton

(insert fire and flames here)

A call came into the firehouse.

(insert fire and flames here)

The cremator is turned on. He was a large man, so they had had to charge more. More gas needed in incinerate the body. So far business as usual. Then suddenly. Cardboard boxes burst into flames. They should never have been there. He gasped. He couldn't just go in there to extinguish them. It was so hot it had made the cardboard-paper spontaneously ignite. The fire began to spread. He rushed, like most places, they did have a fire extinguisher. He rushed to put it out. The heat of the cremator was very intense.

The flames jumped up. He had to get out. He was powerless to the incineration. He didn't know what to do. And that was that. He turned and ran. Ran through the in-house morgue. There they lied, or what had been them. Earthly vessels you could say. They were dead, of that there could be no doubt. That was as unquestioned as it is that Campbell's is a soup company. Nevertheless, still. It felt wrong. Leaving them. But, he rushed out. They were dead anyway.

Alarms rang out. There was a memorial service in progress that morning. The funeral director conducting the service assured them for a moment that it was just a false alarm. But only for a moment. The undertaker ran in.

"It's out of control!" he shouted.

(insert mule picture here)
Houston•Barrow•San Francisco•Upstate New York•Boca Raton

"What?!"

"Something went wrong performing a cremation. We've got to get out of here!" he said.

People panicked. They got up, scrambled for the exits. All rushing out at once. A very smart mouth boy knew that you couldn't yell fire in a crowded theater. But, yelling theater in a crowded fire?

"Theater!" he shouted.

Of itself a petty matter, but it didn't help. Chaos and confusion weren't really quite the right words to describe the scene. Then or now. People knew where the exits were. They exits signs were plain and there was an exit built for the coffin to easily be loaded into the hearse just to the left of the podium. But, it really was spreading fast. Smoke was beginning to waft into the chapel. The alarm was very loud. All together it gave the overall feel and impression of being trapped in a burning building. Trapped and cornered. Panic ensued. And the formentioned exit, instead of being a release, and escape, so they didn't even have to go back out the parlor (lobby) and out the front. Instead, it acted like a thumb over the end of a water hose. In this fire no one was actually trampled, but there were pushes and shoves. Injuries and bruises. And while there were no full tramplings, there were cases of people falling down and even being stepped on.

(insert fire and flames here)

We arrived. It was a weird case. But fortunately it wasn't like weird, horrible-horrific. Just, weird, bizarre. Like that time a flea market burned down (ha ha). I could smell

(insert mule picture here)

slightly burnt coffee. I would later learn that that was really the smell of human cremation. It wasn't that small a building. But there were multiple engines here. And technically it was in West Boca Raton, but we were here as support. There had been some injuries in the evacuation. Mostly relatively minor. There had been people in that morning planning things out in the office. But they got out in time. Building itself was a complete loss. Even a couple of cars in the parking lot a fire engine was having to extinguish. But, all in all. Could be much worse.

We pulled out the heat sensing ray gun. You would think that in a fire you wouldn't be able to tell out body heat. Wrong. It was too intense to go in quite yet. Didn't pick up anything. But as for the back area. That we couldn't see. We went around back. The rear fire exit was open. Guess that was how some people got out. We started to go in, but once again, it was too hot. It was a very hot fire actually. Ended up having to let it burn itself out. I wondered what kind of records were being destroyed. Lost forever.

(insert fire and flames here)

The building was gone. You could tell there had been a building, some posts, walls, vestiges still stood. But really it was a blackened thing. Like bones and artifacts, all that remains of something once great. As much a dead shell as the bodies it had once handled. Surprisingly, no one was greatly injured. The dead however. Normally in a case like this, they will at least return the bone fragments to the family. But in this case, there probably was nothing left.

(insert mule picture here)

> " *It may seem a strange principle to enunciate as the very first requirement in a hospital that it should do the sick no harm* " – Florence Nightingale

Chapter Eleven

It was odd. That last fire. People had run out for their very lives. Fire, flame, dead bodies. Yet, to me it was almost comical. I don't know how to describe it. I guess when you see Jaws and It, then you can laugh at Boris Karloff. Course, I am one to laugh when the monster in the premiere jumps at the audience. Unfortunately as much as I may be fond of him, shall we say, Mr. Karloff didn't exactly hang around for a good long time.

(insert fire and flames here)

The day started out so normally. Almost tranquil. Such is the case always with horror movies. It was later in the day. We responded to a call at The Atrium. An old lady had an episode of ventricular tachycardia, and it could have gone into fibrillation. Now to you that's pretty serious. But to a firefighter, in Oldborough, pretty workaday. Not very strange. And just as there is an Ancient Chinese blessing / curse "may you live in interesting life / times." (I've heard it both ways.) I believe I have dictated how "happily ever after" doesn't make a good story, but it does make a good life. In

(insert mule picture here)
Houston•Barrow•San Francisco•Upstate New York•Boca Raton

conclusion, boring is good. But, as you can probably foresee. This was not a boring day.

For what it was it wasn't that serious. We took her to the hospital. But didn't have lights and sirens. What happened next. I dare not say where it happened. Thought I am sure the locals in the region will recognize the story. And they will know where it must have happened.

We sent in real time a 12 lead EKG of her heart to the doctors prior to arrival through Lifenet®. They were already prepared when we arrived. They probably would have to shock her, but they would sedated her first. Unlike the woman with Asthma might I add. But meanwhile back at the emergency room, we came in. And as you know. When you arrive by ambulance, there is no wait time. Everything was going as-per-usual. Until of course the 7 ½ legged space man from the planet paperback waltz in, said "Hello Lunch!" and gobbled everybody up. Of course that didn't happen (stop laughing). But, where I was. It might as well have.

There is a military saying I have learned from my first boss as a firefighter. While I cannot remember it word for word. It goes something like this "If you can keep your head, when no one else can. You probably don't really know what's going on." Believe me, that's true. Also if you alone cannot keep your head (I have experienced this) then you alone may truly understand what is happening. (or you're nuts, either one could be).

People began freaking out. Something had been communicated to them. I didn't know what. it was crazy. Didn't know what it was. I overheard fire. Then again. What? Really? Whether realism or optimism, I don't know. But I had my doubts. I finally said. Hey, we're firefighters, we can help. Certainly nothing had been radioed in. What was going on? Could it really be? Well, whatever IT was, was not on the ground floor. So up we were to go. Past the patent elevators, right, left, past the main elevators, right, left. Then up a flight of stairs. Shiesh, could get lost in a place like this. But then the frustration died, (following 3 rights and a left). It was an oxygen enriched chamber. Oxygen itself actually isn't a fuel. No, it's a triangle. Usually we have to worry about just one of the angles, fuel. Flammable things. With water we cool, taking away the second angle, heat. But then there's the third angle, oxygen. Ever used a candle snuffer to snuff out a candle? Have it run of air. Well then you're having it burn itself out and use up all the oxygen. It's important enough that in rockets, they have to mix the rocket fuel (one of the most flammable things there is) with oxygen otherwise it couldn't burn in a vacuum.

Now as you could guess, if you increase any of these then it will make things more a fire-hazard. There are chemicals involved in plastics that have to be kept chilled or they'll burst into flames. And increasing oxygen, well. Need I dictate more?

It was an oxygen enriched chamber. And in such a chamber, you can't use a defibrillator. Or, to use the slang "pattles." But they had made a mistake. There is such a thing as a defibrillator that is attached but externally. It's like a life preserver. And somehow a mistake had been made. I have heard of people being sent home with such a defibrillator, but in this case a patent had had one attached. And it had set her (or maybe him don't know doesn't matter) on fire. It was a horrifying sight. A body, seeming dead, certainly unconscious laying there on fire in a clear box. And before my eyes I saw a most horrible scramble-spiral. A male nurse with an extinguisher rushing to save the patent, being stopped. He knew what was happening. He didn't have time to explain, he just had to do. He absolutely couldn't make time. He just couldn't. And then there was the doctor, trying to keep the hospital from burning down. He couldn't let him release the fire and get patents killed. Even an evacuation would kill people. He too didn't have time to explain, he just had to stop him. He too absolutely couldn't make time. He truly couldn't. It was a horrible sight. So often such scramble-spirals emerge in life. In different ways. Always bad, usually terrible. But it's very rare to have one THIS visually apparent. It was only for a moment that I saw this.

SMASH!

It wasn't opened, they just ended up smashing through it. And like that, the incendiary oxygen was released. I jumped back to keep from being burned. Suddenly, there was fire everywhere. The fire alarms were going off. And just like that we had a structure fire. And just about as horrible a one as possible. The boss radioed it in immediately. Faculties such as hospitals, nursing homes, assisted living, in-patent hospice, they have lots of procedures and preparations in case of a fire. I of all people would know. By this point staff were already scrabbling to clear out all the patents. But what were we to do? We were mostly paramedics, I technically both. And had no structural personal protective gear. We had to do something; but this wasn't exactly your normal situation. In a normal fire situation, we'd know better. But we had not arrived as fire responders. We didn't bring the engine so there wasn't much we could do. Many large buildings have fire hoses, so we went looking for one. This was not going to remain a compartment fire; in fact it already no longer was.

We came soon to a surgical suite (or perhaps operating theater is more accurate). Word hadn't reached. As I said, it was now whether the evacuation or the fire itself would kill more people. Oxygen emergency shutoff had already been done. We weren't sterile, but honestly. Surgical suites are not as sterile as people think. There's people in there, people breathing, germs are literally everywhere. It was a brain surgery. But the patent was unconscious. Usually they just give them a local and keep them awake and talk to them so that they can be sure what they're cutting into. Either way. They didn't know about the fire.

He said (being in the middle of an operation he couldn't exactly stop and talk). But he said he couldn't stop he had to keep going. It wasn't quite that brief, but enough that I knew that he knew what he was agreeing to. You see, in rescue. There's something afoot. I can see it. In different things, it's, I suppose. "Don't put yourself in harm's way." Now, believe me. It's not nearly as bad as it is in law enforcement. As they say they just want to go home to their families, and as such they more and more just put themselves first. And become more and more like solders. That spirit of "Our live(s) are simply, inherently, worth more than everyone else's has not spread that far. But, in lifesaving and first aid classes. I see it. Don't get me wrong, it really is true you can't save everyone. But, in what they are teaching, and what kids are learning. I see it. I mention all this because, in that operating room, I saw the opposite of that. It (quite honestly) was one of the bravest things I have ever seen in my life and career.

We made our way out of the neuroscience wing, we were headed back out the way we came in. Down the stairs, past the elevators. Then past the radiology. Where word had reached. I could hear the panic. Our coworkers hadn't arrived yet. But it was clear that we were with the fire department. The top banana of radiology shouted at us for us to please come help. We rushed in, a man wearing 2 backless hospital gowns (one in front and one in back) with an IV sticking out of his foot limped past me on my left. An old lady was quickly pushed out past me on my right being pushed by what I guessed was either her grandson or possibly her great grandson. She seemed utterly clueless to what was happening. It was by this time the fire alarms had long been going. We went into an MRI area. They couldn't open the vault door till they turned the big magnet off; but you know how in all the TV shows, there's a window they're watching through over a control panel. Well, guess that's an accurate stereotype. I could see the patent really freaking out, going back and forth. Like she was trying to escape.

"What's going on in there?" I said.

"Must be struggling against-" said the technician.

"What? She strapped down?" I said.

"There's big padding in there; it's to make sure they stay in place," he said.

She looked panicked. Being trapped in that thing. I know that they are not hooked up to the fire alarm. Ideally they'd be required to have them linked, if it goes off. It spits the patent back out like a vending machine that won't take you dollar bill. But, she just kept struggling and struggling. She must have been so scared. Then, she stopped. I kinda breathed a sigh of relief. Thinking that she had relaxed; and / or knew we were here getting her out. Then it clicked with me; she must have passed out. Soon they had the magnet off. I went in and picked her up. The rest of us there did similar things throughout radiology. I (with her) headed back out the way we had come in through the emergency room. By this point other firefighters had arrived. One in full turnout gear was stopped by an ER nurse saying "You can't go up there with that oxygen tank!"

I said to her "It's just compacted regular air! Trust us. We would know!" Frankly, some things. You just can't think clearly through.

It was soon after that I finally got her out. I didn't know what was wrong. But then I suited up in the proper gear for fighting this. Then I went back in. I wasn't part of extinguishing; no they had already deployed the hoses for direct attack. Err, they were past where I was at any rate. At this exact point I know not for sure if the hoses actually had reached the second floor.

I went back in. 2 nurses rushed someone that had just had a lumbar puncture out on a gurney. A security guard (or maybe one of the cops that's always in a hospital, now I don't remember for sure) was (forcefully) escorting an insane man out. Was babbling something about "stealing his gray matter." Also clearly didn't know I was a firefighter.

Whatever; didn't pay much attention. Wasn't where our platoon was headed. No, we were headed back into the thick of it.

The second time back it was easier to maneuver the turns and staircase back up. (Already knew the way.) As such we got there faster. And by this point they were spraying water directly onto the fire. Being the absolute top priority; they got there faster.

I knew what I had imagined. People lying in hospital beds and cautiously stepping out from their rooms, fire and flames. People crying out for help. The oxygen exploding. Patents trying to shove aside burning sheets, struggling to get out of bed. Crawling; looking for an escape. Well, you get the idea. Fortunately no; I must hand it to whoever was the emergency coordinator for the hospital. They prepared well.

But no! Wait! I wasn't the first to hear it. In fact I was the last to be able to hear it. It was coming from down near where I had been the first go-around. Had it spread to the neuro-operating operating theaters already? We headed down that way. But no. Not to the operating theaters. We stopped at the surgical center elevators. From there it came. It made little sense. Why didn't they ring as a stuck elevator? Because admittedly if you're in an elevator and the fire alarms go off; then it sticks. It doesn't simply go to the closest available floor. But why didn't they push the button and us receive an alert through the radio? How exactly did they know? The alarms. That must have been it. They certainly were going off; must have panicked them.

Quickly we started prying the doors. That of itself was quick work. Problem was, it barely was on the 2nt floor at all. Worse, wasn't down; it was up. There wasn't really enough room for a small person to squeeze down; except maybe a very small person. And I didn't know if it was going up or down, and while firefighters, it's good and intended for them to know a little bit of everything. A thyssenkrupp mechanic I was not.

So it was up to the 3rd floor. And the stairs were, shall we say, not in the next room. Or just down the hallway either. So finally by the time we got back up to the 3rd floor, time had passed. Once again we pried the doors open. I was nervous we might pry open the wrong doors; we didn't. There he was. Patent headed down for surgery. And then I saw it. An oxygen tank. The last thing we wanted to see. There are air concentrators. I've seen them advertised as not having to lug around and deal with big heavy oxygen tanks. But also, not having a condensement; has a now-obvious benefit. Why they didn't use something like that, why that isn't default. Beats me.

"Can we leave that thing behind?!" said one of us.

"No! He's completely dependent," said a surgical nurse.

Also what we didn't want to hear. He needs it to stay alive; but we could all just see it, well. Need I create fear of what never even happened?

The first thing we did was help a large nurse step up and out of the elevator. Then we helped them lift the entire hospital bed out of the elevator. They passed us up some equipment. Then we gave them a hand up and out. It was out of there from there. Fortunately it was on the 2nt floor. Not the 3rd floor. Or, maybe just mostly. But so far it had seemed the emergency oxygen shutoffs had works fine and been successful. Nevertheless, we did have to do a go-around to get out. Having to take the oxygen with us

"*Being brave means to know something is scary, difficult, and dangerous, and doing it anyway, because the possibility of winning the fight is worth the chance of losing it*" – Emilie Autumn

(insert mule picture here)
Houston•Barrow•San Francisco•Upstate New York•Boca Raton

Chapter Twelve

Leaving the hospital all the while fearing a conflagration was not fun. But I left with all my fingers and limbs. So can't complain.

(insert fire and flames here)

An top open island freezer display shorts out. It stops cooling the meats and begins to smoke. At first the customers don't notice. From behind in the refrigerated dairy case a worker restocks milk. A customer decides to ignore his cardiologist and makes up his mind by buying both kinds of sausage. A mother refuses to buy a variety pack of sugary cereal. A Jewish man picks up his smartphone and then promptly blocks a junk call from someone in need of remote access to his computer. Nothing out of the ordinary. No one suspects a thing.

"Mommy! Look at that!" shouts the over sugared boy; more excited than frightened.

"Honey, mommy, please," she says, trying to concentrate on price per egg.

"I've never seen that here before!" he says.

"Sweetie, what is it?!" she says grudgingly and exhausted.

"They built a fire right in the store!" he says.

"What?" she says. Not knowing what is going on, she finally bites, and turns to look.

(insert mule picture here)
Houston•Barrow•San Francisco•Upstate New York•Boca Raton

"Waaa! Fire! Help!" she screams.

The fat bypass patent looks back from the end cap of pork and beans. The Jewish man puts down a box of Great Value saltines and goes running for an extinguisher. The stocker looks up from Borden's. He's worked here for almost a year. Primarily restocking perishables. But not entirely. And in those 11 months 2 days and 93 minutes he's come to know the grocery wing of the store like the back of his hand. He sees that it's true. And it's spreading fast through a display of Bounty 2=4 pack of two paper towels that his best frinemy set up late yesterday. He quickly pulls a rolling in-refrigeration cart of organic milk back and aside and quickly bursts out the clear glass door. While the Jewish man was running for an extinguisher he saw in men's clothing; he stocker knows where there's a closer one. Within 10 seconds he's at the tuna pouches. Would have been half that, but on the turns he would have his feet slip out from under him. In less time he's back with a large ABC extinguisher. Quickly he sets it down without pulling the pin. He quickly points the tube at the display. This was his first mistake.

He thinks "*Maybe saving the store will help me land a promotion,*"

(insert fire and flames here)

The alarm rings in. A fire in a 1300 – DEPARTMENT STORE. It's a call outside of city limits. Officially Wal-Mart is banned form inside Boca Raton. But we do have K-mart and Target. Also they get around it because as was the case with this store; it was legally not in Boca Raton. It was considered unincorporated area; like much of the city. I recognize the area. I figure it must be Wal-Mart. Mid-day. After lunch hour. Not much traffic.

(insert fire and flames here)

The stocker squeezes the trigger on the extinguisher. As you may know, Bounty 2=4 are pretty light and fluffy. They're not heavy. When bringing home a large multi-pack. The issue isn't its heaviness. Instead it's that it's big and awkward. Also (obviously) light things are more easily blown away. This is the issue behind paperweights.

The fire wasn't very much in the refrigeration device. No one has noticed that it's busted and that hundreds (or possibly thousands) of dollars' worth of meat is spoiling. No one has really noticed what started the fire. One person theorized someone was smoking in the store and dropped a cigarette butt. But so far no theories have been spoken out loud. The stocker sprayed the display of paper towels with the extinguisher long and hard. It had spread pretty fast. You see it was a display of paper towels that's wrapped in cellophane and / or shrink wrap and / or plastic wrap. Whatever you call it. It's that plastic outer coating that everything except books and produce seem to have. And even at that; coffee table books are still sold with it. In case you're a little confused. It's that plastic wrapping that had that annoying static cling so it sticks to things after being removed without any adhesive. Well that catches pretty fast. Might as well have been a display of individual toilet paper rolls. Each one wrapped up in that way with that paper that individual toilet paper rolls always are. (one of many things I have never understood; but I digress). And I need not tell you how well paper burns. Sure it's not quite fast as one single sheet of paper burning all by it's lonesome. That has extreme surface contact. But this, it's not quite as whiz-bang (to plagiarize terminology from my father.) But an entire roll will burn longer, (and being more fuel also will produce more heat.) But enough over-brainy-ness.

The fire extinguisher sprayed the burning paper towels away. Like a man with a gun emptying his clip. He just kept spraying at the display. Covering it in fire extinguisher foam. Their outer layer of plastic had burned off (well, had for many of them; not all of the display had gone up into the indoor bonfire). They were blown this way and that. Like chaos theory. Two went up against the metal bottom of the egg display and burnt the rubber buffer. Another went off to a Lays® baked potato chip display on an end cap. It ignited the cardboard of the bottom box wherein the bags of chips had arrived at the store. The stocker, not being a real fireman, hadn't been much paying attention to the rolls going hither-thither. He simply thought that "*stuff will fly hither-thither,*" and really didn't give it any more thought. He concentrated on the paper towel display. Finally it was all coated in fire extinguisher foam. He thought (correctly) that that would restrain and suffocate any further fire. Thought he remained unaware that it was the freezer that actually had been the starting point. Or even that it wasn't working. He really didn't give it that much thought. Narrowly he happened to notice the formentioned end cap display. He turned his head and actually gasped. He knew (correctly) that the bags in and of themselves would burn quite well and fast. Like paper. He rushed over (mere steps) and began spraying it down. The extinguisher ran empty. Fortunately it was just then that the other man returned with the men's clothing department's fire extinguisher. An apparel clerk had briefly held him up. Just in time together they put it out. Like the first bonfire, it was sprayed down thick and heavily. But unlike the first, nothing was flying off. The stacker even ripped bottom boxes open in case the combustion had steeped through the cardboard. In one case; it had. Narrowly, it was put out. Or perhaps "Narrowly" was the operative word.

He let out a sigh of relief with a "phew!" and said "That was close. And something that bad. And that less freestanding. Would have been much harder to put out."

"Could have lost the whole aisle"

"Yeah Dude, well, technically, it's the shelves, the aisle is what you go down. Boss always likes to point that out."

The fire alarm then brought them out of their distraction. You see, all the while they were extinguishing the I'm-pretending-to-eat-healthy-and-stick-to-my-diet-chips. There was another roll. And (if you'll pardon the humor) the roll rolled. Many rolls went all over the place. Most all went to somewhere pretty much free standing and threatened little. 3 different cases admittedly 2 rolls landed together, and burned together. But like the rest they'd simply burn themselves out. Also most had at least some fire extinguisher foam on them. The few exceptions have already been mentioned, except one.

The exception went farther than any other, and was shot straight ahead. It went right up to a little paper sign dropped into a metal frame on a smaller display. Problem was, it was for a sale on Coleman® disposable propane tanks.

By this time the grocery manager had finally arrived.

The sign had ignited, and so had some of the cellophane that was wrapping the Coleman® disposable propane tanks.

"IT'S GUNU BLOW! RUN FOR YOUR LIFE!!" screamed the restocker at the top of his lungs. His scream was heard all the way in bicycles. Everyone heard it. The Pharmacist. The cashiers. People buying orthopedic shoes. Even a man using the rear restrooms after eating spoiled cheese.

The grocery manager was stunned "Run For It!"

It was the lull of the day. It wasn't quite as empty as the middle of the night. But it was too empty for mass hysteria. Still, what customers there were (and the employees) poured out the fire exits. Some, simply went for the main entrances exits where they came in. Not smart knowing how to get out only as how you got in. But, there were not so many people that it clogged up. Frankly, I suppose it simply was a good time for a fire.

They began running faster as they heard weird noises. It began to sound like a full airport with all the propane canisters lighting up. One person mistook it for a mass shooting. But the propane tanks themselves were not what was so bad. Behind the propane tanks, was a display of bottles of lighter fluid in plastic jugs. On the metal shelves next to this was fire starters. Fire shot out of the propane canisters. The lighter fluid was turned into an inferno. Fire starters popped loudly, sparks flew. Obviously other merchandise was set on fire. The first was right there in that double-aisle. Tents, tarps, boxes of stakes. Next was the next aisle over. More camping supplies. Knives, multi-purpose tools, freeze dried food, and other outdoors items all went up in smoke. A bin of plastic tent stakes dripped both off and through the metal bottom shelf and onto the floor. On the other side, the heat of all that burning fuel baked a cinder block exterior wall.

The first area to burn since the chips outside of camping was an aisle of candy at the rear of grocery. A large fire starter spark shot out and was a direct hit on a box of Air Heads Candy Taffy 90 Count Variety Box Assortment. It smoldered, technically still burned. The spark fell down into the bin / shelves below onto a bag of assorted sugar free candies. The plastic crinkled and smoldered. But the spark held in long enough for it to light. The plastic packaging produced thick black smoke. The candies began to melt; their wrappers burned. The fire soon spread to the other bags of candy. Under the metal shelves, molten junk food oozed through the holes punched in the metal. Flames reached up, and began to combust hanging packages. As they dripped down from the heat of their own fires it did somewhat smother and coat the fire in the bulk sizes below.

(insert fire and flames here)

We pulled up. The store was well evacuated. They had cameras amundo to prevent 5 finger discounts. As such a security guard was able to tell us that the store had been well cleared. It had begun in the middle of perishables; but the nucleus was in camping. When he said what was burning, we realized it was inferno enough that it probably would begin to make its own air currents through the store. We quickly hooked up the hoses to the nearby plug. And I don't mean the stereotypical kind synonymous with a dog peeing. No, this was one specially put in just for the event of something like this very thing happening. You've seen them; an FDC allowing us to hook into the building's fire sprinkler system. As with literally any use of hose the engineer had to be careful not to pull out too much water. Deal is, our equipment is so strong that city water mains have been broken because firefighters sucked too much water out of the lines.

After the hoses were hooked up, we went in. The fire had engulfed the camping area, there was a fire in the candy aisle. A door had been left open in dairy, and then we realized we had not properly sized up this Class B fire. It was reaching for the paint department; we had to get out fast. Most firefighters have has some moment wherein they think that this is it. This was mine; I began whispering under my breath. And I could overhear I was not the only one calling on a higher power

We went out the nearest exit. Quite literally running for our lives. Not a moment too soon. We started hearing popping. Explosions. We don't go in with explosions. We did a quick roll call. Which mostly just consisted that we all were out of an unsafe area.

The radio went off. We had not only to get out but away. Next to the paint department was a wall, it was expected to collapse. They were rushing people off the roof. They had been put there to drill holes. The hope was that it would let out smoke, let heat rise out so it wouldn't be such an inferno. But now it was too dangerous up there. And to make matters worse; there was celling support beam right in the middle of the paint department. This was bad; this was very bad.

After that we were to go to the rehabilitation sector.

"Stephanopolopodopolous, you're working rehab?" I said.

"Yeah, come on, I'll check you first," he said.

"I'm fine, course, that's what a college said after a knife fell on her," I said.

"You feel ok?" he asked.

"Yeah, you," I said.

"Can't complain," he said.

"I good?" I said.

"Yeah, you're fine. Go sit down, get something to drink," he said.

"There's nothing more dangerous than a resourceful idiot" – Scott Adams

Chapter Thirteen

That fire would rage on, it was a long fire that went on for a good long time. The wide major aisles would go on the serve as fire breaks. Amazingly no one was hurt; though one person had to be rescued from the bathroom. Nevertheless; sure wasn't fun for us firefighters.

However, was mild compared to this fire.

(insert fire and flames here)

It all began at a bad time. We were taking care of a homeless boy I will call Simon. I had always felt sorry for him. He came from a strict household. He escaped; sorta. Too many rules, too strict. No freedom. And the son they wanted; they made him into anything but. I may have agreed with them on most all of their end goals, but they just went too far and made it such that he simply needed to breathe. And to do that was things neither I nor they would have approved of. They loved their son. But they didn't love who their son was. He just put on a good little act. Few times the true self surfaced (or he tried to open up) it backfired and he quickly had to hide who he was away. I have deliberately not said their or my end goals; or what he turned to. I felt sorry for him. In time, having to change clothes, sneaking out. All the secrecy. He ran off. Like I dictated, they loved their son, but not their son's true inner-self. There is a BIG difference.

How he ended up in Boca Raton; I shall never know. He came from a flyover country / heartland city with a name you may or may not recognize. Knowing about the Dave / Gabe horror. I felt more sympathy. It may not have been legal, but I looked after him as best I could. Different things. Today I hadn't seen him for quite some time. If it had been another city I might have thought he ended up dead. Often he would just disappear and resurface. I never ever knew anything about those incidents. I guess having to hide most everything about yourself and pretend to be someone you're not makes you pretty secretive.

The reason I bring up what is by all rights a personal matter in what I intend for to be strictly about my professional life, well. It was the only time ever the Simon and my career intersected. Simon had gotten something infected. As for going to the emergency room. Minors can't just go in and receive care without a legal guardian. Sure there is John Doe's showing up in an ambulance. But that's about it. All hospitals have to treat if it's life threatening. But this wasn't. The only way Boca Raton Regional Hospital could have to treat Simon is if it developed into blood poisoning. Give it enough time; and what begins any little petty infection can become systemic. President Calvin Coolidge's son died of a blister. But, the Boca Raton Fire Department has advanced beyond the days of Old Betsy. And so such has health care.

I am 99% sure that it WASN'T ok for us to just quietly give him treatment sans paperwork, sans everything, except antiseptic. But, like I dictated, after the Dave / Gabe thing. They were pretty easy going. And I explained some of this; my coworkers; they just did. And if CFO Wood, or Deputy Chief Woodside or John Luca or any of the other Big Wigs read this and then take disciplinary action. Well then I can guarantee that they will personally get a ghostly foot a choice of places. Yeah, I'm dying. Big whoop. Though I worry about Simon, course, pretty much on his own any who.

(insert fire and flames here)

"Boca Raton 911 what is your emergency?" said the operator.

(insert mule picture here)
Houston•Barrow•San Francisco•Upstate New York•Boca Raton

"Yes, Yes help. His face is drooping and his speech is slur-" said a woman.

"Ut oh," said the operator.

"Do you have an available ambulance?" said the woman.

"Oh yes, yes what is your location?" he asked.

"The Debbie-Rand Memorial Service League Gift Shop but, they won't send out a stretcher, they-"

"And what is the victim's age?" he asked.

"He's 87," she said, "But, should I give him aspirin?" she asked.

"Oh No, No, no, strokes, it's either a clot or bleeding, in which case aspirin would only make it worse," he said.

"Oh, well is there anything I can do?" she said.

The operator coughed and said "Well for starters you can give me his name."

"His name is Otis B. P-" she said.

"OH NO!" vocalized the operator.

"What? You know him? -" she said.

"No, No, No-" he said.

"You don't know? Have you dispatched the ambulance?" she said.

"No! No! I Mean It's Real!" he said.

"What's real? What do you mean?" she said.

"I Mean That The Alarm Is Real! I Smell Smoke!" he said.

"WHAT?! What do you mean?!" she said.

"Oh God Oh God, this is bad!" he said.

"What? But, but you're 911! I called you!" she said, hoping that the panic in his voice was fake "I this some sort of joke?!"

"EXACTLY! This Is Bad! This Is Bad!" he said.

"What Is This?!?!" she all but screamed into her phone.

"I've got to get out of here!" he said.

"What?! NO! Help me! PLEASE He's Got A Weak Arm!" she said.

(insert fire and flames here)

"Well, I'm pretty sure your mother would just be glad that someone was taking care of her baby," said a paramedic.

"You say that as though he is her property. So often I hear that about after a tragedy. 'Someone's child' 'Someone's daughter' When young girls get caught up in degrading things. I'll hear someone talk about 'that's someone's daughter up there dancing naked.' As if some father having his daughter doing that is actually worse than that a human person is-" I said.

"Pah! I'll say it again. Pah! No, she'd be furious. She would specifically want not for someone to take care of me; she'd simply want someone to ship me back home. Probably the legal requirement anyway," said Simon.

"Well that tells me all that I need to know about her," said Stephanopolopodopolous.

"Now this will hur-" said the paramedic.

Then the alarm came on.

"Wh-" said Simon.

I quickly shushed him. I am not one to hush and shush people like that. And I certainly felt bad about doing it to someone like Simon. But, it was important.

"Sorry, Fire, have to go," I said, very fast as in passing. Like any other situation, we immediately sprang into action

"*6500 Congress Avenue? Could it really be?*" I thought.

(insert fire and flames here)

We were expected to arrive first. We did. In one way as firefighters it was easy to put out. We all knew this place already. Almost like if we were responding to our own house being on fire. Well, I guess that metaphor (or is it slimily? This is my first time writing. A literature professor I am not) well, I guess that metaphor is more accurate than I first realized. You see, it was the Fire Administration building. I realized that it was real when I saw the smoke coming up. Surprising, hard to believe we of all professions would let it get like this. Seemed like one of those fires where it's a bit of time before emergency services were called. Like if someone has to find the fire first. Well, I guess when you yourself are the dispatch; it's a little hard to call for help and get fire crews dispatched. But, it's not like the whole building was engulfed.

The first person we saw there wasn't even one of our own. Or an operator. Or even a public employee at all. Instead it was a completely panicked woman from Hollander

Sleep products. Some people completely do not know how to handle a fire, I would know. I do this sort of thing for a living (well, technically the past tense might be more accurate. And to the silly-smart mouth-hairsplitter; I am not an arsonist). Well, there went Colormate.

When the fire began they were in the middle of a CERT class. *"Finally!"* I thought, thought that they had ended that. Well, regardless. That was evacuated. As was all non-essential personnel.

First things first, we hooked up our hoses. The engineer set everything up, and being deployed was easy, was a familiar place. We charged the hoses, then went into the fire danger area. It was essentially a boiler room. Flames shooting up; thick heavy smoke everywhere. Naturally we had clean air, but, this was bad, this was really bad. We began putting out the fire, but then. It was realized. They hadn't evacuated. Now, if they had been trying to hook up equipment so that calls could have been transferred out, this I would have expected. It was one of the operators. No, he was under the table, talking on the phone because of the smoke. Didn't even have access to his computers, all the dispatch equipment was up on the desk.

Deal was apparently, well. There are no foreign embassies in Boca Raton. But there is a Brazilian Consulate in Fort Lauderdale, must have driven up from there. Because a consular vehicle apparently got into a fiery collision on Butt's Rd leaving Tiffany's. I don't know just how bad it was, but I expect pretty bad. Those vehicles are considered to be the soil of a foreign embassy, and they cannot be ticketed. Yeah, I know that diplomatic immunity is so that our people will also have it in crazy parts of the world, to protect against trumped up charges. Nevertheless, if you don't have to obey traffic laws, well. What do you expect?

Meanwhile at the burning dispatch, flames were streaking up the walls, but not for long. Like I said, as fires go it was a pretty easy call. Most of the victims and those needing evacuation were professionals. They of all people could handle a fire. Soon we had it extinguished; though the fire damage was severe to that one room

"*Where there's smoke; there's fire*" – Common American Saying

Chapter Fourteen

It wasn't the first time we had responded to a fire at this location. It was a large apartment complex. But the fire wasn't in an apartment. No, there was one building that was larger than the rest; it wasn't an apartment building. Instead it was primarily self-storage. There were also other forms of storage on site. But, that's not the point. The last time we were here, there was a fire in the strip center. It was a cooking fire in the restaurant, but altogether not too bad. This was much worse.

It had begun some time back. Around 3 in the morning they noticed things getting knocked out on the 3rd floor. All security equipment whatsoever was knocked out. They had a security camera going down every aisle of every floor. And similar all throughout the complex. Fire and smoke, burglar, surveillance, everything went out. Officially the company that-shall-remain-nameless had a 24 hour 1-800 number. Unofficially, it was after hours; and honestly on both ends. They said they'd send out a technician in the morning. And since there was no clear sign of anything amiss and by then their shifts would be over and they wouldn't have to deal with a technician. They didn't much bother about it. In the main complex there were a few security guards out at all hours. But in the self-storage, they weren't. They had at least one at any high traffic time (mostly for those going to store their junk to see them on patrol). Otherwise; they were only when summoned. They dispatched one to go check it out. He did a quick glance late that night, missed it. And that was it. There was no fire watch.

(insert fire and flames here)

An early-bird came in early one morning to retrieve camping supplies for a camping trip. He parked in the rear lot, having trouble telling the storage from the parking. He lived within sight; but it was more convenient to have the car nearer the door. It was only one floor up and he was on a health kick, so he didn't even bother with the elevator going up. He opened the door and when he would have been remembering that he really should have taken the elevator with a cart, he instead smelled something. It took only a moment for him to recognize the smell. Smoke! Thinking that that was odd, he decided to go back down, but also give an F.Y.I. as well as grab a cart.

It wasn't immediately that someone came to the front desk. Being as it was around 5 o'clock in the morning he probably was the only non-security person on duty at the time. Even at that he had come in very early for a personal reason. Just as he was about to leave the employee arrived at the desk. First time he had come to that desk in nearly 3 years of storing there for any reason other than something in some way involving rent. Well once regarding junk in with the bill, but only once as he paid ahead.

(insert mule picture here)
Houston•Barrow•San Francisco•Upstate New York•Boca Raton

The man took the F.Y.I. and told security. They looked all throughout the second floor, but saw nothing.

The man removed his stuff all the same; but all-the-while he could have sworn he smelled smoke.

(insert fire and flames here)

An older couple went up to the storage facility. They weren't happy about it, but they were planning to move their stuff into a bigger unit. The rental salesman took them up to the top floor. When the elevator doors opened they were hit in the face with a cloud of smoke. They coughed loudly. It was unexpected and spontaneous, suddenly they were lost; they couldn't just go back down the way they had come in, they struggled out through the smoke. Coughing and choking, struggling to breathe. At least the young salesman was able to crawl on the floor, that helped a little. But they were old, it was painful, they just couldn't get on their knees, not even if a cop had ordered them with a gun could they have. They stumbled, struggling for air.

"This Way!" shouted the salesman. He knew the way; he knew the whole building like the back of his hand. Fortunately there was a stairwell right next to the elevators; the only non-fire-escape stairs within the building.

They struggled and eventually found the way out and into the stairs. Upon entry they gasped and started breathing deeply. Like someone's first breath after surfacing from the water. If that hadn't have been there; it would have been curtains for them.

(insert fire and flames here)

(insert mule picture here)
Houston•Barrow•San Francisco•Upstate New York•Boca Raton

We arrived. We had received a report of an extremely smoky 4th floor. But we knew that that was simply smoke rising. We were able to determine the fire was on the 3rd floor. We hooked up our hoses and we went up. Soon we were on the 3rd floor. And it was roaring. We were up there to try and put it out; but we couldn't open any of the corrugated steel roller doors. Not because they were locked; no we're the fire department, we can get into anything. No, it's the same reason that you put your hand on a door to see if it's hot. Can't open it to fire.

Stuff was burning and crackling loudly. Things popping and breaking. The doors rattled and were both banging and being banged on as if the fire was trying to get to us. Also you see in a campfire sparks going up; same here. Stuff shooting out and overhead, spreading the fire. And that most things in self-storage are in cardboard boxes makes it easier for it to catch. Of the building itself it was made mostly of concrete and metal. There was no concern of it burning down. But everyone's stuff would be ruined. On the whole, heavy smoke, loud noises, extreme heat, and combusting materials flying and floating around. It was altogether like a burning haunted house (worked one of those too).

BANG—PSSSSS

A hot water pipe for the air conditioning system burst, the fire sizzled where it was hit with the water. I will not bore you here with a description of the inner-workings of air-conditioning, if you like turn to the appendix. If not suffice to say that this building used large-building type air-conditioning. And the water pipes were a necessary component.

I similar sound was made when we began spraying over the corrugated steel walls into the units.

I could hear a loud scraping sound behind me. I still don't know what that was. All I know was that it must have been something collapsing, and / or falling over. And as it did so it was most likely scraping the wall of a storage room; but possibly something else in there, or maybe itself.

We were making progress; they were sending up another platoon. But then they heard an explosion. It was later found that someone had put something into their storeroom they shouldn't have. As I believe I have already dictated; when we start hearing explosions, we get out. We were the only people in there, no one else in any danger.

(insert fire and flames here)

Soon we were back in. We went in further. Deeper. Past the loud fire. What had exploded was actually a fire extinguisher, I think I have already explained this. But with the medicines I am on right now. No telling. What was put into the storeroom that shouldn't have been made a lot of heat, and it was just on the other side of a corrugated steel wall, from a fire extinguisher. Sound's crazy, but pressure, heat. Eventually it bursts.

One of the duties of a firefighter is to try and determine the cause of a fire. We did. We found the security controls for the floor. And, copper wiring is better than aluminum. Aluminum causes fires, it expands, it contracts, also causing wiggling. Things can get loose, can make sparks. Sparks cause fire. But copper is much better about not doing that. However the one thing about aluminum wiring is that at least it will expand and contract together. But a mix, that's the worst possible. Aluminum will go back and forth. Copper doesn't like a stick in the mud. A much greater spark risk. Well, the security

(insert mule picture here)
Houston•Barrow•San Francisco•Upstate New York•Boca Raton

box was made with people with safety in mind. They used copper wiring. But the building itself was done on the cheap, they used aluminum wiring. And the box was permanent, by all rights a part of the building. It was not plugged in, it was wired in for its power supply. Of all the things to start a fire. That's also why the floor was knocked out.

"*The world is a dangerous place to live, not because of the people who are evil, but because of the people who don't do anything about it*" – Albert Einstein

Chapter Fifteen

That fire went on for a while longer. What had caused that explosion (beyond what I have already dictated) was that a fire extinguisher came to have too much pressure. May sound ironic, silly, even crazy. But it's true. Already it was contents under pressure, but extra heat, extra pressure. Everything has a pressure limit (well almost everything). Wait, have I already explained that? I'm getting confused.

(insert fire and flames here)

(insert mule picture here)
Houston•Barrow•San Francisco•Upstate New York•Boca Raton

It was all around a perfect storm. In many ways literally. It all began with a tropical depression. Being a peninsula jutting out into what is perhaps the middle of the most hurricane prone part of the world. Florida is not unfamiliar with hurricanes. And Boca Raton being on the outer coast of the Floridian peninsula. We are neither. It was the last day of August. So it was high hurricane season. No, we did not have a hurricane. No, there is a classification system to all this. You have no doubt heard of the 5 categories of hurricane. But, for those of you living in Phoenix or Salt Lake City or Nome. I will briefly explain the lower end of the classification system. For it to be a true hurricane, winds must be at or above 74 miles an hour. The faster the higher the hurricane category. Below that it is a tropical storm. But, if winds are not at least at 39 miles an hour than it is a tropical depression.

We had had a tropical depression and it was bad. Many of our most low-lying areas flooded. These things are gauged by wind speed, but that isn't all there is to it. Also there is other factors to be factored in. Like rainfall. This was one of those storms. Now a tropical depression, normally it's not that big a deal. Normally it passes away on its own, or it forms into something bigger. Well this one didn't. It made landfall as is. There have been plenty of thunderstorms in different places that that were not hurricanes, but did cause flooding. And from a common man's perspective, we had just had a REALLY bad thunderstorm.

The fire engine had trouble making it through the flooded streets. It wasn't so bad we couldn't get there. But it was difficult. Different alternate (not optional) routes had to be taken. Naturally that delayed us. Us and 2 different other engine companies arrived at the scene at virtually the same time.

When we first stepped out of the apparatus, we were standing in water.

Simon (you remember him) I had him and some of his acquaintances (people he knew at any rate) ride out the storm in my residence. It's worth noting that I had cleared my bank books and other personals sensitive items out of my residence before then. But at that moment, any remaining ex-post-facto-it's-only-a-tropical-DEPRESSION concerns evaporated.

Also, the water wasn't exactly as cold as you would expect. Let me explain.

It was (cliché as it is) a condo building. One of the largest in the city. Boca Raton's soil is such that basements cannot be built. And this building was possibly the closest there was to any basement in the city (maybe). It was called an underground parking area, but its ceilings were more than twice as high as depth in which the basement went into the ground. Many basements have basement windows, a small window up high in the basement, but down low to those outside. But here you could simply duck down to get in through them, Then jump straight down several feet.

The basement had filled with water, but it was also on fire. You see, there had been an attack by a disgruntled person. He had dynamited the sprinkler system and lit cars on fire using streams of gasoline used as fuses. As I have discussed, a room built with all modern materials takes only 2 minutes to become engulfed in fire. And without a sprinkler system, you can imagine how quick it could spread up to all five floors. We hadn't been able to get in at all. So it was burning out of control. I might call it a fuel controlled fire; except that to those of you outside of my profession, that would imply that there was any control. There wasn't. Clearly it had been planned for the worst possible time. In many cases you've seen the stereotypical case of people in a high rise building with their heads out the windows shouting "Help" and "Save my Baby!" Well, this was it.

The building was really two, sorta three. Within the block there were 3 buildings. And there were roads, or possibly alleyways running through it all forming a T. The two condo buildings were rectangular, elongated but side by side. And at the top of the T was another building. The other building was smaller, and a floor shorter. Underneath it was the only part of the block that didn't have parking level under it. So it was more like 2 stories shorter. It too was rectangular, but it was with a smaller footprint. Some of this may be worded oddly, I'm aware. Thinking about it all, let's just say I don't like to.

Meanwhile back at the condos, it was hard to get close, the gasoline had ignited basically the whole basement; there was far too much water for it to simply boil away; no that would be too easy; but there was plenty of fuel and burning cars to heat the water up. Up enough that we couldn't close.

It was fortunate that one of the responding wagons was the latter truck. The fire was spreading fast, our priority was rescue.

My first rescue was very stereotypical. It was a young small woman on the lowest dwelling floor. First she handed me her baby, then her other baby (twin girls). It was so scary going down, if I dropped one, they'd be dead. I handed them off to a paramedic, then went back for her. Her apartment was bright red, it was engulfed in a roiling raging fire. It was hard to hear over the roaring, everything was engulfed, not much was even discernible. Even within my turnout gear, I could feel the extreme heat coming out the window. As I let her down I heard the sound of a window break, or perhaps burst would be more appropriate. When I put her down I looked up and saw flames shooting up out of windows. Just in that little bit of time, it had gotten worse.

Not everyone was sticking their head out a window. Many ran to parts of the building that wasn't on fire, or perhaps not on fire yet I should say. There were fire escapes, ways to get out. But not everyone had had time to get out in time. Some got trapped.

And like I dictated, there were two buildings. And this side, this one. We were the only ones trying to rescue. The good thing was that it wasn't higher than 6 stories. It's pretty universal that city fire departments cannot latter rescue above the 6th floor.

Soon other fire engines arrived. Like, latter trucks and others better equipped to handle the crisis. All the while the fire had just been spreading. We saved a good fair number of people that day. But, we had to prioritize. All the worst incidents I have responded to in my career we were terribly overwhelmed. Way too little manpower. This was a great example. But, they came. And quickly. Never feels quick, believe me. I'm sure it's the same feeling the soldier has when he hears "air support 30 seconds." But I digress; enough of that.

It was when we got relieved by backup; in many ways that was when things really got hard. You can see that there are so many in danger. Literally in this case screaming for their lives. But, you can feel overwhelmed. Or you can see that you've pulled people from a burning building and feel good. I will explain:

This is no doubt a story you have heard before, I've heard it more than once I know. But, I will tell it again nevertheless

(insert fire and flames here)

There once was a boy in the beach. He saw that starfishes had washed up on the beach; while he was certainly not a marine biologist, he knew that if they stayed there, they'd die. He also knew that they couldn't get themselves back into the ocean. So, he picked one up, and threw it in the ocean. He then grabbed another, and threw it back in. Then another and another. Eventually someone came along and asked the boy about it; about what he was doing. He replied that he was saving the starfish. Well this person was a pessimist such as myself, and pointed out (truthfully) that a LOT of starfish had washed up. The beach was covered. So, what difference could the efforts of one little boy make? Well, the little boy heard these words, bent down. And picked another up. And again tossed it into the ocean. Then he said "Well, made a difference for that one."

(insert fire and flames here)

But I ask, what if the boy wasn't there? What if the boy had been grounded? What if (hardest at least for him) he had simply been sent to spend time in his room and stare out at the starfish drying on the beach in the sun?

The other building I was somewhat surprised hadn't already ignited. Well, it hadn't. But (quite obviously) it would. It would ignite. We were sent over to the other building to evacuate it. I was surprised they hadn't already. I do admit that they had at least been on call and gotten themselves a little ready to clear out; but that's about it.

The other building, I have stepped around and gone out of my way. I have not said what the other building was, I believe that I have said that it was not housing. But I believe that that's all I have said. It's something, and I know that this will get me ridiculed by many of my readers. But it was something that I don't like to think about. I wish I could just skip over it all. I can't. Why lie? It's basically the crux of the chapter. What was that building I am sure you are wondering? That building was the Palm Beach county juvenile courthouse.

I was not happy about having to even go in that building. Now I know that many of you will call me anarchist, and other things I do confess I do not want to listen to. But, enough about me. I recognize the necessity of many of the darker parts of society. But, when (and I have known minors caught in this cycle) a boy is raised without a father. He goes out and finds one on the streets. He gets into trouble. The judge becomes the mother. And like a political commentator returning hatred for hatred. The cycle is played into. In some world's children are born into getting into trouble with the law is simply to be expected, juvie is inevitable. And they just lock them up. No one really tries to help them, sometimes positive programs even are shut down by lobbyists representing correction's industry and jailor's unions. And the cycle is played into. The delinquents, instead of being loved are hurt, and they are made better criminals (you know, jail is collage for crooks) and judges and prosecutors and Etc., they are never prosecuted. Life just goes on. And they never say their sorry. You get what I am saying. It all just steamrolls over like a brovdingnagian juggernaut. Meanwhile the general population simply hears about their crimes, they get scared, they hear simply that arrests have been made, and they are safe. Never think about the plight of the accused. Even those that are sympatric, rarely do anything. Like a good friend illuminated to me "Deadly collision on the freeway. Oh Great! Better take back roads!!" There are other legitimate concerns to be had, such as how people, "well, if they're guilty. That's what matter. If it takes a 7-8-9 hour interrogation to get a confession. I don't care. I'm safe." But, I digress.

We went in, I wasn't happy to have to be one of the ones to have to go into that place (well that wasn't a tortured sentence now was it?). But I was. It was pretty clear that they didn't get the real fire danger. Like I think I have dictated, I was surprised the building wasn't already on fire. But it wasn't. We were in turnout gear, though not with the air tanks when we went in. I don't know what rigamoreroll they had to go through, but even in that moment, they STILL didn't get it. I've heard of similar things happened at the pentagon on 9/11. Couldn't get them to get out. Put in tear gas, they put on gas masks and Still wouldn't get out. Man, I really should have reported myself. My heart was going so fast my cross training told me I was going to pass out. My last fire in Madison was flashing through my head. Was it to happen again? Could it really? And for what?

Well I must give credit where credit was due. They did get out. Everyone. Only very minor injuries. We left and went back in. This time fully prepared. The condos were now receiving from Miami Fire department, the Kings Point Fire Department, the Delray Beach Fire Department, and the Boynton Beach Fire Department. I still don't know why we were the ones not just going in there, but back in. Oh well, on That Night. We just did and did and did. It broke so many regulations it would make your head spin. I don't know how we got so many out that day in Madison. But. Nevertheless. Guess it was a bit like that.

But when we came back, we could tell they were FINALLY clearing out. Fire alarms were sounding, people were being escorted out. It had crossed my mind (though I don't know just how many procedures it would go against and laws it would break) that we would have to go in and turn the fire hose on the authorities. Imagine that, law enforcement Being Hosed Off! Well, that never happened. But, I did see things. Things I could by all rights not bear to see, yet I did, I had to. Things which the world needs to see. And I mean see as in "see the light of day; see the sky is blue" not just see and perceive.

Among other things I saw a boy. At first I thought it was Simon, but then I realized that he looked notably different and had to have been someone else. And I remember what he said "You Think You're So Much Special?! You Think You're Above It All! You

Think Your Authority Is Absolute! Well It's Not! You're Not…" That's all I caught. And it hurt. He was struggling, the cliché case of the person being kicked out, and brutally manhandled. Can't fight back and being tossed out. But instead it was fighting for freedom. Now I'm not saying he was innocent or wrongfully accused, or anything like that. I knew not anything of his case, still know nothing. Was just some subordinate minor on trial. Struggling for freedom, quite literally. Who knows what he did or if he should have been free (once again, not an anarchist). But struggling nevertheless. And the cops, they could make no sense of what he had to say. Even if they wanted to I am sure. Though I am sure that they didn't. I am not saying that he is right. Giving my most fair assessment from what I saw and know, I'd bet he was 80% wrong in what he had to say. Certainly didn't help that he wasn't able to be calm. But that the cops only made worse; stopping the bleeding from a stab wound by simply shoving the knife in deeper. But, nevertheless, still what he had to say was to fall exclusively on deaf ears. No one is all correct, but when things are so utterly dead-set a certain way. Well, sometimes it takes a far out lunatic to stumble across truth. As the platitude goes "a stopped clock is right twice a day." It took all I had in me to not do something to those law enforcement that no man is ever supposed to do to another man. I felt like I was that boy, they were hauling off the starfish to the drunk tank to dry out. And I was grounded to my room in the beach house; only to watch.

But enough about that, there were other such things I saw, but on second thought, I think less is more.

Perhaps the worst part of it for me was actually how close it was to a different incident much longer ago. When it happened, I was just a boy.

It was late one night, nearly 9ºClock close to closing time at Westgate mall. Some young kid, not a teenager. He had been shoplifting. And I mean seriously. It was so stereotypical. He tried to get away, it was such a powerless joke. I mean he really was a kid, and he was really freaking out. But the cops were just trying to move him along and drag him downtown. Naturally the mother was freaking out, saying stuff like "Why Is He In Handcuffs?" and "Where Are You Taking Him?!" You can imagine. Cops simply gave her "that doesn't concern you." Err, something of that. She ended up being tazered. Man that kid was so scared. Kind of freak out if it had happened at school, there'd have been no living down. I did nothing, I was a kid. Nothing I could do. Yet still, one thing sticks with me "I Did Nothing" I always rebuttal it when it comes to mind with "There was nothing I could do." But still, sometimes, it sits there, takes up a fraction of my mind.

Sorry, like I said, fraction of my mind, sits there, my mind keeps going there.

We pressed ahead. We knew there was a fire, and we knew that the bailiffs that worked there knew the building better than we would. I tried to fixate on the fire. We were led through the courthouse building, till we came to a large set of doors. As firefighters we knew they couldn't be opened. But an idiot bailiff, almost as a kindness, a politeness, opened them for us.

What happened next I confess I was glad to see. We've all seen in the movies where the fire bursts out when the door is opened. Almost like a swimmer coming up for air. Well that's exactly what happened, the fire was released into the corridor. We knew better and jumped back, it missed us. But the bailiff was flung into a wall. We turned our hoses onto the bailiff to extinguish his burning uniform. I will not lie, after seeing the ruthless handling of the underage accused, I was glad to see him suffer. I wasn't happy to be glad of it. I didn't revel in it, but nevertheless. Also I did not let it affect how I handled my duties. I consciously went out of my way to make sure it didn't. (maybe I succeded). Good, evil, or both. He was badly hurt. We would have to take him down to an ambulance. The fire would have to wait. But I did do one thing. I looked back, into the courtroom. Excuse was to make sure there wasn't an accused shackled and dying in there. But I saw it. I was surprised with my technical knowledge it was so intense. There was no one in there. But the fire. It was a typical / classical courtroom. Everything make of deep and rich wood. A large symbol behind the judge. Etc… At least so it seemed. Everything was on fire. And I mean everything. The entire room. A bastion of authority, a corridor of reprisal. Where people could come to plead, literally. Now it was the powerless one. The sword of justice cutting both ways. I know, ultimately it's a room, a creation of architecture. But still, the place was truly consumed. Maybe it's the idea, the principal. Guess I can get quixotic. And to make matters better we honestly and legitimately couldn't fight the fire. Like I dictated, we had to get the bailiff to an ambulance. We left. We fireman carried him out.

Upon leaving the courthouse, we saw that there were more firemen there to combat the blaze from Fort Lauderdale Fire Department. We had already radioed details, but there were other parts of the building going up in flames. I also saw the condos. The two buildings were both now with much more fire engines there combating the fire. And the buildings themselves had progressed as well. Now they were both an absolute inferno. I have heard of warehouse fires, and chemical plants. But this, it was simply the buildings in and of themselves. I even got to look in between the buildings. It was a complete conflagration. Just like in the great Chicago fire. The buildings had begun burning collectively in a massive inferno. It was not a bunch of different fires. But, our first priority was getting the bailiff to EMS.

After we handed him off to EMS, we went over to recovery. We had done enough.

"Stephanopolopodopolous! I was half expecting you to be there when we carried someone out from the courthouse," I said.

"You had to carry someone out of the courthouse?" he said.

"Yeah, a bailiff. Didn't understand about checking if a door is hot," I said.

"This your first courthouse fire?" he said.

"Courthouse, yes. But, not my first juvenile corrections fire," I said somberly.

"Oh," he said, then after a momentary pause, it clicked with him, "Oh! Oh, I'm sorry, this must be-" he said.

"Don't mention it. And I mean that! I don't like to think about it either," I said.

"Sorry," he said.

"Meh, how you holding up?" I said.

"This isn't my first courthouse fire; first was in Houston. Not even my first courthouse incident here in Florida," he said.

I turned my head in that way dogs do when they're confused.

"Yes, first call out to this courthouse, or these condos for that matter. But it is not my first call to a courthouse. First one was right before you arrived here in BRFD. Was the main county courthouse. Where they were checking people. X-raying stuff. You know, like at an airport. But, this one woman. She had to walk with a cane. But they had to take the cane from her, I think to X-ray it, maybe to metal detect her, not completely certain. Well, she truly couldn't walk without a cane. She fell; ironically hit her head on the conveyer for the X-ray machine. And got a mild concussion. Don't think it even made the tribune."

"*The fisherman know that the sea is dangerous and the storm terrible, but they have never found these dangers sufficient reason for remaining ashore*" – Vincent Van Gogh

Chapter Sixteen

A soccer mom turned east onto East Palmetto Park Road off NW 1st Ave. She realized she should have been on N Dixie Highway, and headed the other direction at that. The traffic light turned red and she stopped almost a foot short of rear ending a big white car.

"Ugh! Traffic!" she said exacerbated. She was having a really stressful day.

"Kids please, Mommy's trying to find it, let mommy concentrate!" she said, trying not to lose it.

Ding! Ding! Ding! Ding! Ding! Ding! Ding! Ding! Ding! Ding! Ding! Ding! Ding! Ding! Ding! Ding! Ding! Ding! Ding!

She had stopped on train tracks. The lights began sounding.

That scared her. The other driver wasn't paying much attention.

"Come on!! Come on!! Just run it! I have to go!" she said, knowing full well she couldn't be heard.

"Ut oh!" said the daughter.

"Should we jump out?" said the boy, as much to the girl as the driver.

"Honey! Mommy! Please!" she said flustered and panicked.

Ding! Ding! Beep Ding! Ding! Beep Ding! Ding! Beep Ding! Ding! Beep Ding! Ding! Beep Ding! Ding! Beep Ding! Ding! Beep Ding! Ding! Beep

She turned her head and saw it.

The driver of the white vehicle was not realizing what was about to happen; was simply too engrossed.

The girl unfastened her booster seat belt, the boy pulled the car door handle.

"Kids-Sit-Down-I-Got-This," she said fast all the while blowing the horn.

Ding! Ding! Beep Ding! Ding! Beep Ding! Ding! Beep Ding! Ding! Beep Ding! Ding! Beep Ding! Ding! Beep Ding! Ding! Beep Ding! Ding! Beep Ding! Ding! Beep Ding! Ding! Beep Ding! Ding! Beep Ding! Ding! Beep Ding! Ding! Beep Ding! Ding! Beep

Both children climbed out of their booster seats and went to get the doors or windows open.

"WERE FINE SIAT DOWN!!" she said in a flustered, frustrated, panic. The children were scared back into their seats.

Then the train made contact.

(insert fire and flames here)

(insert mule picture here)
Houston•Barrow•San Francisco•Upstate New York•Boca Raton

We were responding alongside other first responders to a simple train wreck. I know how the word simple must sound in this context. But, I suppose it's like comparing the loss of shoplifting to multi-million dollar executive embezzlement or comparing a liquor store being knocked over to a mass shooting.

It began rather mundane. Once again, comparatively. A car had stopped on the tracks. Train came. Triple fatality. We could tell that the 2 children in the back had tried to escape. Investigators assumed they couldn't get out because the child safety locks were on. I know, sounds like a horrible and heartbreaking accident. But, well, you'll see.

We were working the scene of the accident. In fact the engineer of the train had already inspected to make sure the train was safe to go on and had left. We ourselves were getting ready to pack it up and leave. Some of us already had. Not, not all of us. Still not sure if that was a good thing or a bad thing. Buy, it was nevertheless.

Then all of a sudden, I heard bells sounding. I looked and the lights were flashing. Now we've all seen this, nothing out of the usual about it. Except this time. This time it was like Tommy Knockers. But we didn't know it. What was about to happen was one of the deadliest collisions in U.S. history. Certainly in the history of the City of Boca Raton.

A gas tanker made a right turn west towards a 7-11. Though it couldn't have been making a re-fueling there. Wasn't any pumps to need a reservoir refilling. The driver noticed the lights and stopped, albeit in an intersection I might add. This was one of those railroad crossings right next to an intersection. Almost with one on both sides, though the intersection on the other side was a much smaller thoroughfare. Palmetto Park Road more passed it than intersected it. You know the type. The side street has to look both ways, and the major street can turn off, but doesn't have to stop or yield.

Someone ran up and started shouting. Shouting at a cop. We didn't listen; probably wasn't time anyways. But, the cop took him down and began arresting him. Not sure what for exactly, probably he freaked and committed assaulting an officer. Whatever it was, was not really important in the grand scheme of things.

And I know that people will read this and think that it's anti-police. Well the deal is simply that cops are humans and humans are stupid. So was how the squad car was parked. I have long imagined that that arrestee was shoved into the back of that cop car and no doubt was trapped, a death trap. However it has clicked with me there wasn't time for that to have happened.

But it might as well have.

The train by all rights rear ended the squad car. Could just as easily have been a fire chief's wagon. (SUV) Makes no difference. Still, that was just a mere domino. Of itself no lasting consequence.

We of all people should've known better; we should have learned our lesson after the derailment of a Tri-Rail commuter train. I was part of the frantic search. But between the false reports of fire and no fatalities. I guess that wasn't enough.

You should never attempt to cross train tracks unless you are absolutely certain you can cross. And you obviously should never park on train tracks. I guess the officer had thought that he was far enough back. But, the train rear ended him (trains overhang the tracks by a few feet in either direction), shoved him forword. Shoved him right into the gas tank underneath the door to the fuel tanker.

As for the train collision itself, I was unharmed (so far). I was on the other side of the tracks, and I was not far from it. But also I was more towards the direction the train was coming from, so I guess that that must've been protection enough.

But it had only just begun. Just then we realized just what we were in store for. I saw the flames and the fire through the passing train cars. I saw the tanker. I realized it. And the train cars, I know from training they can be carrying things so flammable that you can't put water on them. It'll make it worse. I feared it might be that. Though it proved to be a crude oil unit train. Well, bad enough.

As the arms had gone down, two school buses had pulled up. They were carrying little kids. As such the students were small in size and more could be crammed into a bus. Me and other firefighters rushed at them. Shouting warning. They had to get out of there. Yet, now, all this time. I've wondered. What if instead they had backed up and floor-ited down (or up) 1st Ave? Could they have gotten away? Couldn't have ended any worse. Those buses were built with 12 benches on either side. And they were absolutely packed. Only one child survived. Even at that, was so badly disfigured probably would need for a school for the blind to make him an exception. I'm not joking, no school will really do what it takes to stop the bullying. Certainly not a public school, no their priority is their union pension. But enough about that. Frankly I think this whole book may be a distraction from the guilt of my mistake.

I quickly got the back door open, we told them to run for it. But, the bus had (much much smaller) fuel tanks of its own. And outside they were utterly out in the open, exposed.

They ran, I rushed them, more and more. An all-fired-panic. I wanted them to be panicked, for them to run faster, for them to get to safety. I knew what was to come. When a gas tanker blows up, it's like a bomb going off. But, when an entire train goes off. I just kept working, that I didn't think about.

Then it went off, the tanker truck detonated. The explosion was massive, I still have no direct memory of it. It destroyed a Hebrew supermarket. And an old large Buick full of old ladies headed out for bingo was right behind it. All four of them died. I assume that the convenience store was damaged; but with all this. It's so hard to quantify what was the truck, and what was the train.

For all the magnitude of an entire fuel station refill lighting up; the train was greater. But unlike the truck, it was not all at once. Instead the train was a bunch of little, no little is most assuredly the wrong word. The train was a bunch of individual explosions. Each one greater than the tanker truck. And it was like dominoes. After one, it was powerful enough to cause those next to it. Some of the train cars had already passed it, and the line of explosion quickly followed. The train engineer knew what was happening, barreled out and ran away. He survived, but not everyone on the train. As for the majority of the train, that hadn't passed through the intersection. They were headed right into the epicenter of it; but it came to them.

The train explosion destroyed two different gyms, a 7-11, an optical place, a bank, several restaurants, police headquarters (what is it with law enforcement and my career?) and countless other places. Just the force of the blast even destroyed at least one building that was never even ignited. I don't even know how many places were destroyed. I believe the death count all totaled was 147, but I am not sure. I know many of my firehouse were killed. Don't even know who all and how many. I fear I am the only survivor. Well, I shouldn't dictate that. Not really accurate. I'm dying, I know it. I was in full turnout gear; but still by burns were horrible. Are horrible. I hope this book is somewhat accurate. I'm on a lot of medicine. They found me under one of the school buses, probably shielded me somewhat. With plenty of injuries consistent with being hit by a vehicle, but. Burns are the most important. Frankly I'm surprised I've made it long enough to write this; err, at least dictate it.

Obviously I have not responded to ANY calls since this. This was and will be my last fire. But, still. I do not think I will rest in peace. What about Simon? What will become of him? Sure, I haven't done much. When he would find me out, or I ran across him I'd run in someplace and see to it that he didn't go hungry. I haven't done much, but I'm about as much as there is in terms of anyone looking after him. What about Dave's trial? I was to testify, it's finally coming up. He's been sitting in jail all this time. But, I'm sure I won't live to see it. My manuscript, I've talked to people. Hoping to have more copies made. But how? There's only one left. Even if I could arrange it to happen; what if something went wrong? Then it would be gone forever. And all that's assuming it will be allowed in court. At least the defense attorney knows about it, though I don't know if he's any good or just a fulfillment of the right to an attorney. Who knows. About that I have also lost sleep. But the drugs they give me help me sleep. I have other concerns as well regarding my passing. Personal matters that need no mention. However those 2 are two top concerns.

Not really sure how to end this; this is the last chapter. And Now I am finishing it up. Guess I'm done. I've long remembered everything in this book. I knew what I wanted to write. But, I didn't think I would get this far, I really didn't. So, I have had no final end in mind. I don't know just how to end it. You can stop taking dictation now.

Appendix

(insert mule picture here)
Houston•Barrow•San Francisco•Upstate New York•Boca Raton

Chapter Four

Have you ever noticed how water and oil mix? They don't.

They reason they don't mix is that they don't bond on a molecular level. Now something that would mix with water, say flavor powder. That does bond. How? Well water isn't (forgive me I'm a firefighter not a physics teacher, might be errors or wrong terminology) molecularly balanced. It's like a stronger and a weaker child with something they want. Say a toy, but more likely a video game nowadays. The stronger, meaner child will get more time on the console, or whatever. Same with the big mean strong oxygen and the electrons flying around.

This is also how water bonds to water. One oxygen is getting too much electrons, on another water molecule, there's a hydrogen that's not getting enough. So it naturally passes it onto the hydrogen. But, like I dictated. Oil is balanced. Messy, but balanced. It can't (unlike drink mix) jump into this interaction. This is why oil and water do not mix.

But, gasoline and oil are both balanced. So they can. And as you know, oil fires are very hard to put out. Yes, water actually can put out an oil fire, but it took 500 gallons dumped from a helicopter. And gasoline is a quick lighting accelerant.

That's what was going on in downtown Madison.

Chapter Fourteen

It was a big apartment complex. It wasn't really an apartment tower; it truly was a complex. Lots of buildings scattered across the campus. The outlying ones were only 2 stories. But the inner ones were 3 story apartment buildings. However in the center was a 4 story building. It had the largest overall footprint of any building on the complex; but also it was not an apartment building. Instead it was self-storage, and a lot of it. You see, in front on the 1st floor was a strip center. On the far right was the leasing office to the whole complex; or perhaps front office would be more accurate. Because catty corner to it and occupying the whole center of the 1st floor was office space. Not just for the complex, but also additional office space that was leased out. Also in there was where the complex security was located. The office led to 2 different hallways.

One hallway ran alongside the edge of the building and led straight to the back of the building, where the main elevators and entrance / exit for self-storage were located. Behind that was parking for self-storage and auto / boat / RV / Etc… storage lot. Next to that hallway was a long elongated space for people (tenants of apartments and self-storage alike) could leave large items (such as furniture) for other random people to grab.

The other hallway was much shorter. It led to a private post office. It was full service. With multiple carriers, as such places usually are. Though it didn't sell the packing material; that was sold primarily for the self-storage and only in the office in order to make room for more mailboxes. Also it had P.O. boxes; though once again, as a private post office, they could not be differentiated from apartment mail boxes by senders. In fact that post office was where the apartments' tenants received their mail. Each tenant was given one box for free; and the self-storage tenants were offered it at a discount. However in the formentioned hallway there was a door. It was one of those doors like in pictures in nursery rhymes and in nursery-babysitting areas. That is the door could be opened like any other door; or you could just open the top half, talk to people, and exchange items. The door led to the offices of the complex newspaper. That is assuming it could be called that. From an architectural standpoint, it simply led into the vast office space. Beyond that it was sectioned off strictly by cubical, the kind you have to walk around, you can't reach over. There even was an intentional gap soasto allow you to walk from the journalist's office to the main complex's office. The newspaper was weekly and placed in every mailbox. Also it was sent out to self-storage tenants along with their bill often times (though billing was monthly; so it would be simply the diseur). Also it was available in newspaper dispensers throughout the complex. And in every store front in the strip center, except one. Even was available in the self-storage elevators next to the seat for those that couldn't stand for the whole ride and elevator banks.

Beyond all that was a restaurant. It was barely not losing money (or perhaps it was simply not losing much); It marketed itself almost exclusively to those in the complex. It was international; a little bit of every-thing globally. Also it was simply a cheap place to eat. It was a subsidiary of the complex and was the only business endeavor undertaken that did not involve leasing something.

Beyond that was an empty space. At one point it had been considered for being subdivided up (as they expected in construction) in order to lease it out for retail. But the company backed out of opening up there. And that was that.

After that was what was on the far other left end of the strip center. Officially it was two different things. Next to the empty space was a laundry shop. It was essentially freestanding the laundry aisle of any number of stores. Only more focused on laundry than general cleaning products. Sure there were a few snack items and one small rack of books. But that was it. There was the shortest hallway between the two. It was practically a doorway. On one side the large panes of glass of any strip center. And on your other side was a booth serving both. Washers were throughout the washateria. But driers were only on the far side along the outer wall for the sake of exhaust. The washateria was even elongated, going farther back than any other in the strip center (though not to the back of the building) so that all the driers could be along an exterior wall.

Floors 2-3-4 were all simply self-storage. With the exception of one bathroom per floor by the elevator bank, stairwell / fire escapes, and etc… it was nothing else.

Also arguably there was a 5th floor. The roof itself had non-climate-controlled self-storage. That is, where there wasn't air-conditioning units.

On the whole, it was a large building.

(insert fire and flames here)

As you may know, there is no such thing as cold. I think I may have already explained that. Deal is, that while you can use a furnace to create heat. You cannot create an anti-furnace and make cold. Also you can't destroy heat. What you can do is dissipate heat, or in this case transfer it. Your refrigerator and your air conditioner work on the same principal. They use a gas in coils. First they take the gas once it has been heated. Well, ok that's the part of the loop process that I'm jumping in at, none are as good as any other I don't think. And run it through a compressor. That's also what uses up the most of the power. It compresses it down into the dissipation coils. Can't guarantee that that's the correct term. Not an HVAC tecnition. But, it compresses and squeezes that gas into the heat dissipation coils, much like wringing out a sponge. The gas through the coils gives off heat. Then in it is back released. And for so much space it naturally expands to, so, so much heat it can hold. Much like a sponge as well. It takes on more heat. Then it is taken to have the heat compressed (or squeezed) back out again.

However on a larger scale air-conditioning system (such as the one for the self-storage building) it uses a different model. Everything I have just explained still applies.

(insert mule picture here)
Houston•Barrow•San Francisco•Upstate New York•Boca Raton

But it is being compressed into water. The heat that is. And the building as a whole, just as all the individual air-conditioning systems have decompressed cooled gas coils, and compressed gas coils releasing heat. So the whole building has cool water pipes bringing water to different coils to receive and remove heat. And hot water pipes being hauled off to usually a roof to either be cooled off or simply released as steam.

43512998R00086

Made in the USA
San Bernardino, CA
14 July 2019